Ryan

Journey of the Spirit Man

A NOVEL BY GEORGE MENDOZA

WISE TREE PRESS
Mesilla Park, New Mexico

Published by Wise Tree Press.

Wise Tree Press is an imprint of the
Wise Tree Foundation, INC.
P.O. Box 1243, Mesilla Park, New Mexico 88047.

Website: www.georgemendoza.com

Library of Congress Control Number: 2022933982

To my daughter,

Maria G. Mendoza

Author's Note

In 2011, I had a terrible hiking accident in the Organ Mountains of New Mexico where I live and dream my dreams. I fell a good thirty feet, broke my arm and my teeth. I suffered from cluster headaches for a long time after that fall.

I was lucky to be alive but the cluster headaches were terrible. I saw vivid visions, which I painted and which turned into this story. The headaches and pain led to a wildly productive period during which I painted up a storm and wrote novels about my superhero, the spirit man.

Then, one day, the clusters stopped, but I continued to paint and write books. I guess it's true that a good bump on the head can bring out creativity! I have been accused of living in a fantasy and dreaming my life away. That's probably true, and I would not have it any other way.

Journey of the Spirit Man is the first book of a series.

Acknowledgements

I would like to express my appreciation to Erne Barge; Dr. David Boje; Mindy Byrnes; Louie Burke; Rachel Carrillo; the Castillo family; my art teacher, Imelda Chacon; Bobby Cook; Mayra Enriquez; my sister, Kathleen Firth; Dick Guttman; Janus Herrera; Neal Hidalgo; Anne Hillerman; Craig Holden; Dr. Dan Howard; Sonny Irizarry; Thomas Kindig; Doylene Land; Daniel Landes; Jamie Lapage; James McConnell; Michael Marrufo; my son, Michael Mendoza; J. L. Powers; Robert Rivera; Ron Rowlett and his son, Ryan Rowlett; Antonio Sanchez; Jane Seymour; Mary Sherman; Holly Watson; Thomas Zubia; and others who wish to remain anonymous.

I am very grateful to James Salas and Raquel Ortega with the New Mexico Commission for the Blind who funded this incredible book project. To Jessica Powers and Kathy McInnis who designed this beautiful book. To my agent, Frank Weimann, Folio Literary Management, New York. And to my editor, Shane Inman, the man with the magic touch!

A special thanks to New Mexico State University,

— continued —

the NMSU English Department, and especially the
Creative Writing staff for their help and support in
this and other projects.

All characters in this book are figments of my imagination with the exception of Michael Spirit Man.

George Mendoza
New Mexico

Chapter 1

When Michael ran, he had no need to think about his dreams. The fog-shrouded desert, the watchful eyes, the distant calls to prayer—all of it disappeared beneath the pounding of his feet on sand and rock. He sprinted up the rugged mountain path, vaulted over boulders, and left the unsettling visions far below, in the changeless expanse of the New Mexico desert.

He hooted and crowed as he reached the mountain's crest.

"Top of the world!" He felt drunk with delight at his speed, his power.

Mark, his best friend and running buddy, had stopped to catch his breath some fifty yards back. Michael flashed a grin down on him. He always enjoyed running with Mark because it gave him a point of comparison, reinforced his certainty that he was unbeatable.

"Hurry up, it's great up here," he said.

Mark gasped for breath, hands on his knees as sweat dripped down his tan face, gluing his thick black hair to his forehead. Then he straightened, wiped his brow, and continued on. There was, Michael had to admit, something admirable about Mark's tenacity. Michael couldn't imagine what it must be like to be Mark, to struggle every step of the way and keep going nonetheless. Running had always come as easily as breathing for Michael. Not a speck of challenge in it.

Finally reunited, the two runners rested on a large boulder that overlooked the valley. From their vantage point, high in the granite crags of the Organ Mountains, they watched the shadows lengthen across the desert. To the west lay the green band of the great river valley, the Rio Grande, and to the North, the sweeping rust-red panorama of the Jornada Del Muerte, the Journey of Death. About ninety miles northwest, the forested massifs of the Gila Wilderness lay on the horizon. The river wandered south, weaving its threads of green throughout the ochre sands and the strange lunar blackness of ancient lava flows, toward the mysterious distant mountain peaks of Mexico.

A storm billowed near the horizon, slowly boiling toward the runners. Shafts of late afternoon sun were swallowed up by the approaching cumulus clouds, one by one giving themselves over to the dark.

"Do you know what this feels like?" Michael said. "Like we're at the frontier of creation. Like everything is beginning right before us. Like all that world down there, and all those people, are suspended in time, just waiting for us to come back down from the mountain to bring news from their gods."

Mark chuckled and shook his head, still catching his breath. "Man, you say the weirdest things sometimes, you know that?"

Michael punched him in the arm. "I'm serious though."

The storm drew nearer. A column of thunderclouds grumbled. A cool wind whipped across the mountains, carrying with it the fresh smell of ozone. Michael jumped up as the first few raindrops flecked his face.

"Race you back to the house," he said.

"You really think you can beat me?" Mark said.

Michael flexed his left hand, where a silver ring shone on his little finger. He brought the ring to his lips and kissed it, as he did before every race. "This ring has never lost a race."

"Good thing I'm racing you and not the ring, then."

The two runners took off down the path, Michael taking the lead and setting a driving pace. Mark fell behind all too soon, unable to keep up with his friend's long-legged stride.

"Come on!" Michael shouted as fat droplets spattered the rocks around them. He laughed at Mark's huffing, labored stride.

At over six feet tall, Michael was a wild creature of the plains— his skin tanned from a life lived in the sun, his limbs long and limber and quick. He was the perfect running machine, and nothing else mattered in the world but his feet against the ground, the rush in his ears, the spring-loaded motion of his legs.

Michael's house lay at the foot of the mountains. It had once been quite a distance outside Las Cruces, but the town's expansion meant it now lay along its suburban outskirts. It was a lovely old adobe hacienda, surrounded by giant cottonwood trees. Their branches reached outward from gnarled trunks five feet thick, creating a hollow cupped space that looked like a thousand webbed and tangled hands, each doing its part to shelter the house. Michael and Mark ducked into the house just in time to escape the wrath of the growing storm.

Michael looked Mark over and raised an eyebrow. "I thought you said you'd beat me, but you just look like you're about to die."

Mark's face flushed red. "I'm having an off day," he said, rubbing his thighs.

The two-story house featured a vaulted ceiling with a sunroof, which on clearer days filled the house with light. The thick adobe walls kept it cool in the summer, while the stone fireplace in the living room shed the warmth and comfort of firelight during the long, cold winter nights in the desert.

Mark grabbed two cans of beer from the fridge, popped them open, and handed one to Michael.

Michael's mother appeared, carrying an armful of medical journals, as they flopped onto the sofa. She stopped when she caught sight of the beer in their hands.

"Don't you have a race tomorrow?" she said.

"Yes, Mom," Michael said. "We actually just got back from"—his eyes cut sideways to Mark who was still trying to get his breathing back to normal—"a light jog."

"Light, my ass," Mark said. He took a swig of beer.

"You're not worried that beer will affect your performance tomorrow?" Michael's mother said.

"One beer won't kill us, Mom. I can't possibly lose."

"Well, do what you want, but one beer may slow you down more than you think." She brushed past them and disappeared into her office.

The two men went up to Michael's room. As usual, it was immaculate, cleaned daily by a professional housekeeper. He had the latest surround sound stereo system, a desk with a custom-made triple-monitor PC, and a small library of books he'd never read. Above his bed, Michael had a framed, signed photograph of Charles Atlas, "The World's Most Perfectly Developed Man." Next to it hung a slightly larger photograph featuring Michael in a similar pose.

Mark ran his hand over the spotless computer desk and said, "Do you ever think about how wild all of this is?"

"All of what?"

"All of it." Mark gestured around the room and toward the house beyond. "Everything you have."

Michael shrugged. "No?"

"Right," Mark said. "It's normal to you. To have rich parents who give you everything you want and need."

Michael didn't like his friend's tone. Something was different today.

"Right," Michael said. "They give me *everything*. They won all those races for me. They got a running scholarship for me." He rolled his eyes.

"What I mean," Mark said, "is that your parents have been able to buy you the best running shoes, hire running coaches, pay for your every expense so all you have to worry about is the track and not holding down some cashier job somewhere. And yet you think none of that matters. Like you have no advantages."

"You're just mad about losing our race today."

Mark smiled at him a little sadly. "No. I would have lost that race with or without everything you have. You are special, but..."

"But what?"

"You can't see what's right in front of you."

Michael bristled. "Where's all this coming from all of a sudden?"

Mark paused by the two photographs on the wall and didn't say anything for a moment.

"Wendy called me the other day," he said. "Crying, because you stood her up again. Your own girlfriend, man."

"Oh, that? I just wasn't feeling it, plus I had to practice. What's the big deal? She got over it, didn't she?"

"Other people's lives are a big deal, Michael."

Michael laughed, trying to disguise the fact that he was getting pretty angry now.

"I'm serious," Mark said. "Do you ever wonder why you've only got one friend?"

Michael stared. There were times when he thought Mark looked a little like a rat, living off the crumbs of better people's trash. Now happened to be one of those times.

"Are you kidding me? Everyone wants to be my friend. I just don't have time to be friends with people I don't give a shit about."

"They aren't your friends," Mark stated. "When your glory is gone, all those people yipping at your heels will be gone too."

"Phew, you had me worried there for a second," Michael said. "Passing glory isn't something I have to worry about, thank goodness."

Mark shook his head. "You have no spirit, you know that? Only somebody with no spirit can act like he was the best thing that ever happened in the history of the world. You're so busy appreciating yourself you don't see the important things."

"You're so jealous, you're peeing green," Michael said, bending the beer tab back and forth with his thumb. He wanted this conversation to be over.

"I mean spirit like knowing who you are, not having to feel superior just to feel good about yourself. You have to be dedicated to something bigger than yourself to have spirit. But you? You're only dedicated to yourself."

Michael felt a twinge deep in his gut—was it the beer? Or were Mark's words spot on? But no matter what it was, he wasn't about to let Mark see it.

"And why shouldn't I be?" Michael said. "Haven't I earned a little selfishness?" He motioned to the fully-stocked trophy case by the window. "I'm on top, and I haven't even reached my peak yet. If I can't admire myself, who the hell can?"

Mark shook his head. "Do you even hear how shallow you're being?"

Michael thought back to the past year or two, wondering if Mark could possibly be right. But for as long as he could remember, he had been better than everybody else at just about everything that he did. If there was anything he wasn't better at...well, he didn't concern himself with it. He wasn't interested in spending time improving one stupid skill when everything else came so easy.

"Mark, dude, I'm sorry," he said, "but people aren't born equal. Some people really are better than others. It's not an easy fact to face, but I've faced it, and sooner or later, you'll have to face it too. Remember when we were in high school? I was the one who brought our school to victory. You saw it. How can you say I have no spirit? Or that I'm not actually better than other people? When those crowds cheered, they cheered for me."

"Just because you're a star doesn't mean you have spirit. Okay, so you're a 'natural' when it comes to sports, but that doesn't mean you're better than anyone else." Mark crushed his beer can and threw it in the wastebasket.

"It isn't just sports," Michael said. "Everything we've done together—I've always done it better. School...women...everything. If that's not spirit, what is?"

Mark spread his hands in a gesture that said, "I give up," and said, "Okay, Spirit Man. You win. Again."

"Things come easy for me because I have spirit," Michael said. He felt like he was caught on a loop repeating himself. But it seemed so self-evident. Why were they even talking about this? What was wrong with Mark?

Mark glanced down at his watch. "It's time for work. Sorry, man. I have to go."

"Why don't you find a real job? Delivering pizza for a living is a joke."

"Pretty rich coming from you."

"A year from now people will throw tons of money at me just to hear me name the shoes they sell," Michael said. "Now *there's* a job."

"Whatever you say," Mark said. Then he left.

Michael stepped onto the balcony. The dusk air was cool, the wind crisp. He inhaled deeply, taking in the earthy smell of rain in the desert. A small stream carved its way alongside the driveway. Raindrops cascaded onto the roof, trickling down and falling just beyond the edge of the balcony. Michael reached out his hand and let the droplets spatter cold against his skin.

Below, Mark hurried to his car, skipping over puddles and ducking quickly into his old Volkswagen Bug parked next to Michael's yellow Hummer. The ancient machine sputtered to life, crawled down the driveway, and vanished into the rain.

Michael didn't like the way he felt as he went inside. He dialed Wendy's number.

"Hey," he said when she finally answered after three agonizing rings.

"Oh, hi Michael!" She sounded happy to hear his voice, which made him feel better. "Ready for the race tomorrow?"

"Of course. I'm always ready."

She laughed. Her laugh was like a wind chime in the breeze—soft, tinkling, and pleasant. "Of course you are! I can't wait to see you win."

"You and the rest of the universe." He grinned, suddenly secure again. "So what are you doing tonight?"

"Just spending some time with the family. Do you want to come over?"

Michael's fingers tapped nervously against the phone. He did want to go over, he wanted to see her—but he had a strict pre-race policy not to distract himself. "I better not," he finally said. "I just wanted to hear your voice. I should be getting to sleep pretty soon though."

"Oh, okay," she said. "I miss you."

"You too," Michael said, and hung up.

Michael stared at the trophy case on his bedroom wall, a glass monument filled with countless victories, engraved in gold and silver. He had taken his high school basketball team to several national competitions. In football, the exhibition of his prowess as a quarterback had only been limited by the ineptitude of his offensive line. He had letters and trophies for every major sport. He had one more year of college, and then his life would really begin. Sponsorships, cheering fans, the Olympics....It would all become real, wouldn't it?

Spirit Man. Mark's jibes came back to him as he thought about all he planned to accomplish in life. Sweat broke out on his forehead and upper lip. His stomach twitched and his knees felt wobbly. Had Mark really meant all of it? Even worse, had he been right? Michael tried to shake off the thought. It didn't matter what Mark thought or said or did. All that mattered was winning the next race, and the one after that, and the one after that, and on and on until Mark and everyone like him simply had to accept that Michael Seymour was the best there ever was—not because his parents were doctors and he lived in a miniature mansion, but because he himself was made of something different than all the rest. Those gold medals would belong to him and him alone, and he would have no one to thank for them but himself and his lucky ring.

The rain shower stopped and a calm spread through the valley. The western sky still held a faint purple glow and the mountains on the horizon stood in stark silhouette. This was the track he'd learned to run on, as a young boy. He remembered how it felt to run through the deserts. How it seemed like there were glittering surprises everywhere...ghostly surprises. Even in the bright sunshine, the desert seemed populated with the spirits of people who were long gone or perhaps had never existed at all. They glimmered behind prickly pear, popped up around mesquites. Children making faces at him, mothers cheering him on, dads wagging their fingers at him and smiling. One time, he sat in the dirt and had a conversation with a woman who said she'd been his great-great-grandmother.

Sometimes he had seen other things. A city rising up out of the desert floor. People walking from building to building. A caravan of men leading camels to a watering hole. Visions. Mirages. Definitely mirages. The result of the overactive imagination of a child. Sure enough, as he'd aged—and begun to earn renown for himself as a runner—the visions had grown sparser and sparser still. Eventually, by the time he was winning every race for his high school, these ghostly visages ceased entirely. These days, he wasn't certain what had prompted such wild imaginings, or what had stripped them away. But the desert was certainly lonelier without them, and without Mark.

In the quiet of the growing night, without the movement of his body to distract him, dim recollections of his dreams crept back into his consciousness. A desert enshrouded in fog. Eyes watching from the mist. Pilgrims trudging across the sand. And somewhere, in the center of it all, a great dark space into which he could not see, but from which emanated terrible, agonized screams. All these images beckoned to him in some way he couldn't put into words, but it was this darkness which pulled at him most strongly. Some nights, like tonight, he was afraid even to close his eyes, fearing this might be the dream in which he gave in to that call and entered the dark.

Michael scoffed at his own foolishness and went back inside, to the beautiful, lavish emptiness of his room.

Chapter 2

Ten minutes before his race, Michael could barely concentrate. The right pro scouts were all there, plus media from Albuquerque, El Paso, and beyond. One of his teammates said there was even a reporter from the *Los Angeles Times* in the audience. Everything he had done had led to this. This was where it all would become real.

A small but dedicated crowd had gathered and the name "Michael Seymour" was on everyone's lips, either with adoration or a quiet anxiety murmured by members of the other team. Anyone not cheering for him was being warned about him and he liked that just fine. As the underdog university, New Mexico State was waiting for a miracle, and they had positioned Michael as the saint who would bring it to them. The rest of the team held the line on points. As the moment of truth approached, Coach Morgan trotted up to Michael from the sidelines. A former runner himself, Morgan had given Michael the guidance that had sharpened him into a lethal runner on the track.

Clapping his hand on Michael's shoulder, Morgan said, "Michael, if you were anyone else, I'd be worried right now. We're right down to the wire. We need the points from first place, you got it?"

Michael grinned. This was his moment. Everything rode on this.

"Give 'em hell," Morgan said.

Michael concentrated on his breathing, trying to focus all of himself on the race. He began his elaborate series of stretches that might look bizarre to an outsider, but which made him limber as a twist-tie, able to move in any direction required. He bent over to do some toe-touches, twisting from side to side. He looked behind him to see a rival runner staring at his theatrical warm ups.

"Nice view, huh?" Michael said. "You better get used to it. It's all you'll see on the track."

The other runner scoffed and walked toward the starting position to do some stretches of his own.

Michael glanced around the track. He could picture exactly how he would win. He would fall into the middle of the pack and keep a steady stride at first, letting go those who wanted to get an early lead on him. He would pace himself to conserve energy, then, at the exact right moment, he would give it his all and speed right past the tiring quick-starters to take the lead. After that he would take the advice he sometimes gave some of the newer runners on his team: "Get out in front and stay there until the crowd starts screaming."

Michael visualized all his fans cheering as he brought his school to victory once again. They shone in the radiance of his glory. There were his mom and dad at the side of the track, tears of pride and joy shining clear in their eyes. There was Coach Morgan, beaming as he cheered, "You're the one, champ!" There were the girls, the cheerleaders...and of course Wendy. There was always Wendy.

He jerked back to the present when he heard her voice. She was calling his name from across the track and running toward him, arms wide, a sweet smile on her face. She threw her arms around his neck as she said, "I love you and good luck!"

He was caught off-guard for a moment, her warm body pressed up against his. She smelled great, strawberry with a hint of lime, and her dark eyes sparkled in the midday sun. He hugged her tightly for a second, forgetting all about the race.

Then the outside world slipped in. He heard jeers from his teammates. "Aw, Seymour's gonna get lucky later..." and "Whoo hoo, who owns Seymour's ass?"

Michael pushed her arms away, his face hot. "Wendy, you're destroying my concentration."

"I just wanted to wish you luck." She frowned, wrapping her arms around herself in a defensive gesture. Hurt flashed in her eyes.

"I don't need luck and I don't need this right now," he said.

Her face flushed, confused and ashamed. "But I—"

"Will you just get off the track? This is actually important."

"I just thought—"

"You didn't think, that's what," he said. "I'll talk to you later, OK?"

He meant his last words as a propitiation, something he could use later as a buffer to his behavior or as an excuse. But Wendy looked like she was about to cry as she left, slowly walking off the track and up to the bleachers where her parents were sitting. Her parents looked at her in concern as she sat beside them, then Michael turned away. He didn't need the distraction.

Michael turned to Mark and said, "Can you believe the nerve..." He added a chuckle at the end, something to cover the awkward way his stomach turned. That wasn't good. Surely something so small couldn't throw him off, right?

"Michael, you know she didn't mean anything bad by it," Mark said.

"She should know better. She knows I need total concentration." But he couldn't hold onto his anger. It was true, she hadn't meant any harm. And that was the whole problem. He should be thinking about the race, not about her and some stupid misunderstanding. He knew it was stupid. He knew that afterward he would see her and everything would be okay, like it always was, but now they would have to talk about what happened. Maybe he'd even have to apologize—even when he did nothing wrong—when she was the one who should apologize. She was an athlete too—surely she should get it—but maybe it was different for cheerleaders? Maybe they didn't need to get in the zone the same way runners did? Or maybe they *depended* on interaction, on community, on each other. Ugh! Michael pushed all those thoughts aside. But he couldn't help but glance back at the bleachers and saw that she was definitely crying now.

Mark nudged him and nodded toward Wendy. "I think you should apologize, man. Think about what's really important."

Michael scoffed. The race would start any moment now, and he couldn't afford to waste one more second worrying about Wendy. "She'll be fine," he said. "I'll talk to her later."

A moment later, the loudspeaker announced the 1500-meter race. Michael twisted his lucky ring, positioned himself on the starting line, set his feet on the starting blocks, and waited for the gun to go off. The world around him dropped to nothing as his mind narrowed in on the moment. He was going to win. It was a fact. It was fate. He just needed to step into it.

Adrenaline surged through his body as the gun fired and his legs hurtled him forward like the elastic tendons of a slingshot. Other runners took the lead as he positioned himself in the pack. He calculated each breath, reserving his strength in order to give it his all on the last lap. He couldn't hear the crowd, couldn't hear the wind—nothing but the track was real. His body felt great, like each muscle was full to bursting with some pulsating form of pure vibrant energy.

He began to laugh, to stalk each of the runners ahead of him, planning each moment when he would make them his prey.

What he loved best about this sport was its eternal nature. It felt primal, his ability to run faster than the person next to him, as though he were literally taking part in the great evolutionary race, "the survival of the fittest." Apart from the shoes and the clothes, the sport hadn't changed since the Greek Olympians used it to pay tribute to their gods. It was as old as mankind itself, and Michael was determined to prove himself faster than anyone who had ever lived or ever would live. His speed-breaking record would be eternal, and his name would be praised for generations to come. As long as there were men who ran, who raced each other on foot, the name "Michael Seymour" would be forever remembered.

He pumped his legs, wiping the sweat out of his eyes as he rounded on the final stretch, passing the runner who had been in first place. Now he could hear the crowd, and they were going wild cheering his name. Everything was right in the world.

Then...everything fell apart.

The whole incident took less than three or four seconds, but it was enough. It began as a strange tingling sensation in his lower leg, like he had struck his funny bone. Perplexed, he looked down at his leg.

The pain cut up through him, interrupting his stride. His momentum disappeared. That clear picture of his world, his victory, his fate, slowed and smeared like someone had run their fingers through the wet paint on the canvas of his life.

He pushed harder, but when he looked ahead, he didn't see the track. Instead he saw the mountains and a gate he was approaching fast. His mind couldn't make sense of it. A gate? The mountains? And there, beyond the gate, red sand dunes. Where was he? Where were the track, the bleachers, the fans?

In the next instant, the world began to spin. His leg burned as a sharp pain slashed from his leg to his hip. His legs folded under him and he fell. His knees scraped against the track, and then his elbows and palms, then his chin, each impact cutting deep gashes in his skin, marking his belly with a nice pink rash pockmarked by dirt and grit. The lancing pain in his hip was joined by dozens of other hurts blooming like shots of brightness in his head.

"Oh, God," he cried as he tried to roll back onto his feet.

He willed his legs to work so he could get back up and drive himself back into the pack, even as victory disappeared before his eyes. But his legs cramped so badly he was paralyzed and his vision reeled round and round, a high ringing sound echoing deep in his ears. For a moment, he thought he saw a group of men on camels galloping across the track, which was suddenly transformed into a barren desert, devoid of water, the track, the rows of seats where people sat watching the race. They were dressed like nomads and they were headed straight towards him. Some of the camels hobbled on three legs, some were colored a bright highlighter yellow, and some were tiny, about the size of his hand.

The moment stopped, his vision cleared and, instead of camels, Michael saw the audience, full of people, their mouths making small, round Os in surprise at his sudden fall. He heard cries of dismay in a sea of confusion, his own mind struggling to understand what had happened. Feet pounded the ground around him as the other runners dodged his prone form, flying over him on their own uninterrupted journeys to the end of the race.

He looked at the finish line, arm stretched outward, projecting his mind across the line. But his body wasn't there. His vision blurred and then the earth turned and rose to meet his face as darkness crowded the edges of his sight.

"Michael! Are you all right?" he heard Morgan calling.

There was a lot of noise, but it seemed so far away.

Michael tried to say, "Get me up, Coach, I can still make it," but he was unable to move or speak, only groan.

"Medics!" Coach bellowed. "Someone call an ambulance!"

Michael was barely hanging on to the edge of consciousness when he realized he had lost. He had lost the race. He had lost his Olympics. He had lost everything.

Through a dim distance, as though she were speaking underwater, Michael heard his mother's voice. "We're right here with you, honey," she said. "You'll be all right. Everything will be all right."

He struggled to find his voice, to reach out like a man swimming up through dark water, not sure when he might break the surface, if he ever could. "I can't move my leg," he mumbled. But though he spoke, nobody responded. Maybe he just imagined he had spoken.

He thought about Wendy. Was she still in the stands, watching this? He wished she was here with his parents. He wanted to hold her hand more than anything in the world. If he had to go to the hospital, he wanted her to come with him, to be there too. But would she even come? He'd just told her to go away, to leave. And for nothing.

"Wendy," he croaked, or thought he croaked, but again, no one responded. It was as if he had said nothing at all. Somebody—no, two somebodies—were feeling for his pulse and examining his limbs, his chest. The outside world faded in and out of static.

Michael felt for the edge of the track. He leaned his head over and puked up his breakfast, eggs, and dry toast.

"Loser!" somebody yelled.

A tear forced its way past Michael's eyelid and trickled down his cheek. He left it alone, hoping it would dry quickly, knowing he couldn't lift his hand to wipe his cheeks because then people would realize he, Michael Seymour, was crying.

"Hey, man," a reassuring voice said. "You'll be all right, okay?"

Michael's head began to clear and he opened his eyes. Mark stood beside him, looking down with a strained smile. The haze that surrounded his vision slowly dissipated. The leg convulsions subsided to steady spasms as his leg finally began to relax.

"The race?" he asked.

Somebody interrupted Mark's response. "How do you like that view?"

Michael lifted his head as much as he could. The runner he had taunted only ten minutes earlier turned around, bent over, and shook his rear in Michael's face.

"Get out of here," Mark said, and stepped toward the runner. The runner laughed and loped back to his teammates.

"Don't listen to him," Mark said. "He's just an ass."

"Mark. The race?"

"I was the best in our team and I was fifth. They won."

"Can you get up?" one of the paramedics asked.

Michael nodded and let the tech help him to his feet. For a moment he wobbled, his leg somehow too weak to bear his weight. The paramedic didn't miss a beat, easily sliding her arm around his waist and holding him up. Embarrassed, Michael found himself leaning on the paramedic's narrow shoulder until he regained his balance, gingerly keeping weight off the injured leg.

"What happened out there?" Morgan asked. "You were steaming and then…"

"My leg just gave out." Michael put his hands over his face, then took them away the instant he remembered the spectators in the stands. He had to at least maintain some dignity. Especially in front of Wendy and her parents. Now he hoped they *had* left before the race. Even if he had to apologize like crazy later, he hoped they hadn't seen this.

"It'll be okay, man," Mark said.

The paramedics checked Michael over and decided everything seemed normal. They helped him off the track. The spectators offered the smattering of applause traditional for an injured athlete, but he could tell it was only half-hearted and he was sure he heard jeers from the stands. He gave a faint smile and a polite wave, wishing he could get out of sight as quickly as possible. It wasn't fair; his body was not supposed to give out on him. If he had to suffer the indignity of a hospitalization, it should be as the result of something dramatic, something heroic. He should be a victim of a gunshot from foiling a bank robbery, or a knife attack from stopping a mugging in progress.

"This isn't normal," said Morgan. "I want you to go to the hospital right now and get yourself checked. It could be something more than just cramps." He put his hand on Michael's shoulder and continued seriously, "And Michael, don't let this crush your spirits, okay? There are other races to win."

Michael couldn't even manage a nod. He wanted to believe him but he just couldn't.

Mark and Morgan helped Michael into his parents' car. He sat in the back seat, with Mark on the other side, and they headed to the hospital.

"How are you feeling?" his mom asked.

Michael grunted. He told himself he wasn't sulking. He was too old to sulk. But he wanted everybody to leave him alone. As they sped toward the Mesilla Valley Hospital, he found his thoughts returning over and over to what had happened just before the race. The way his words had cut Wendy. What in the world had possessed him to say those things? Clearly, he *had* needed luck today. And right now, he certainly felt like he needed her. What a strange thought, that he needed another person. Wasn't that what Mark had been trying to tell him the night before?

"I've got to find Wendy," he said. Then: "Is it too late?"

"There'll be another race," Mark said gently.

Michael turned to look out the window. The world was indistinct, abstract. Mark could say anything he wanted, but the next race didn't matter anymore. Michael had lost. He'd lost more than the race—he'd lost his future. Those scouts would never look at him the same again. And Wendy? Even Mark seemed uncertain that she would forgive him.

"Hey, I lost too," Mark said.

Michael only snorted. Trust Mark to try and join this one-person pity party.

As they pulled into the hospital parking lot, Michael tapped his mother's shoulder. "I feel fine," he said. "Let's just go home."

"You've never fallen before," she said. "This isn't optional."

His father pulled up to the entrance. He got out, leaving the car running, and went around to Michael's door. He opened it and held his hand out. "Come on, Michael."

For a few long seconds, Michael sat unmoving. Then he lifted his injured leg and got out, pushing his father's hand away.

Their eyes met.

He wanted to ask if he should be worried. He thought about his grandmother, the only person in his life who went to church, who would—if she was still alive—be lighting a candle for him at St. Guadalupe's just a few miles away. "Our times are in his hands," she would say. "You will be okay." He wanted that kind of reassurance but he couldn't ask his dad for it.

"I'll park and join you inside," his dad said.

"Okay." Michael stifled the words pent up inside.

"It was probably just the beer we had yesterday," Mark said as they walked inside.

"Sure," Michael said, toneless. Or it was the world deciding to end around him.

The rest of the day was a blur. He followed Mark and his mother inside, waited as his mother spoke to the nurse in charge of admittance. When they called his name, he told his parents and Mark to wait. Alone, he went into the small cubicle where a nurse took his vitals and a doctor questioned him about what had happened, then decided on a battery of different tests.

"What'll you do to me?" he said.

"Don't worry. It won't be painful," the doctor said. He looked at the scrapes on Michael's legs and arms and clucked. "We'd better clean these wounds before they get infected. You wait here, and I'll be right back." The doctor gave Michael a professionally friendly smile and left the room.

Then it was tests, tests, tests. Having blood drawn, lying down inside a machine, positioning his leg for X-rays. In between these, he watched doctors and technicians confer with one another just out of earshot. What were they saying? What did they know that they weren't telling him? Was he going to die?

Michael sat alone in these sterile rooms and knew that nothing in his life would ever be the same.

Chapter 3

Evening was setting in when Michael parked his Hummer in Wendy's driveway. He meandered along the walkway that wound through the garden, around shrubs and a bird bath and desert flowers, leading from the driveway to the front door. Wendy's father once told him the complex design was intentional, demanding discipline from the homeowner to maintain. Of course, the one keeping the garden perfect was a landscaper, not Wendy's father.

The front door opened before Michael reached it and Wendy's mother stepped out, arms crossed. Suddenly the warm, inviting landscape lost its luster and seemed dead and cold.

"Is Wendy here?" he said. "I'd really like to talk to her."

"She doesn't want to see you right now, Michael." Her voice had no give in it.

"I...I just want to talk to her."

She was unmoved. "We all think it's best if you just leave her alone from now on. She deserves better than a selfish kid like you."

"I want to apologize," he said. "I didn't mean what I said...I just... I wasn't thinking." He saw the curtain in one of the windows move. There was Wendy, just watching. Was she really going to let her mother send him away?

"Wendy," he yelled. "Please! I want to talk to you! I—"

He heard the click as Wendy unlocked the window. She opened it only a crack.

"What?" she said. She didn't sound very forgiving.

"I shouldn't have spoken to you that way," he said. "I—" He tried to look around Wendy's mother. If he could only get into the house, if he could only speak to Wendy face to face...but her mother was unmoving, blocking his way.

"I cared about you so much," Wendy said. "But you've done nothing

—nothing—our entire relationship except push me away."

"I'm sorry, Wendy, I—"

"I loved you, Michael. But you're too—you have too much ego. You think you're too good for everything and everybody."

"Wendy..."

"Even now, you can't even tell me you love me."

He opened his mouth to speak, the words were there on his lips, but he couldn't release them.

"Goodbye, Michael. Don't call me again." Her window closed with a thud.

Her mother stepped back inside the house, glared at him once more, and closed the door in his face.

He stood there for a moment in shock. This wasn't how it was supposed to go at all. He was supposed to talk to Wendy, work everything out, put things back the way they were before. Part of him expected the window would reopen, because of *course* it would—but it didn't. After a while, the light in Wendy's room went out. Michael, dazed, turned away, back around the bird bath and the shrubs and the flowers.

Night fell on the town as a harsh wind blew across the Mesilla Valley. A haze of dust filled the air as a lonesome wind rolled down from the mountains. Michael drove aimlessly, back and forth, zig-zagging across streets he normally never visited, looking for a distraction. At a certain point, he realized he'd turned onto Mark's street without thinking. He almost drove right past his friend's house, perhaps to a bar where he wouldn't be recognized, but the night was too big and empty and he needed to talk to someone or he might just burst. Who better than Mark, more loyal than a Labrador?

It was a small house in an older part of town, though not a particularly unpleasant neighborhood. Mark had once pointed out, when Michael had referred to the area as "low-rent," that it was more accurately "low-buy." The homes were old and worth little on the market, but many of the residents in the area were owners, proud they could own their own homes even if they were at the bottom of the economic scale.

Michael stepped out of his Hummer and saw Mark sitting on the front porch with his acoustic guitar, watching the windy night with a hint of a smile on his face. His expression shifted to one of pity when he spotted Michael approaching. That stung. Of all people, Michael wanted Mark's pity the least.

"What's up, man?" Mark said. "How are you feeling?" His voice was overly gentle in a way that turned Michael's stomach, made him feel like punching a wall.

Michael sighed. "I don't know," he said. He felt like an animal, chased by hunters—too tired to run any further, lying down, on the edge of accepting defeat. The wind was whipping his hair into frayed mats and his eyes burned.

"You look pretty rough, man," Mark said.

"Gee, thanks, you look great too."

"You don't have to lie just to make me feel good," Mark said with a half laugh. "Why don't you come inside? It's miserable out here."

Mark's father was sitting on his favorite recliner, watching television in the living room. He was drunk, but at least it was a pleasant drunk. The man slurred, "Hey, Mike, how you been? Haven't seen you in a while."

"It's been a day from hell, Mr. Lucero," Michael said.

Mr. Lucero paused, looking at Michael for a bit before saying, "Heard what happened to you at the race. I'm sorry."

The comforting smile Mr. Lucero gave him bothered Michael. He didn't want Mark's father to feel sorry for him any more than he wanted it from Mark.

"It happens," Michael said.

An awkward pause, then he followed Mark to his bedroom, a small cinderblock cell decorated in early Thrift Store. Mark set his guitar on the bed. An old but functional stereo rested on a bookshelf of boards and patio blocks. On the beat-up yard sale desk hunkered Mark's laptop, a battered old behemoth he'd bragged about getting on sale for fifty bucks last year.

Michael sat down on the bed, a double mattress and box spring placed directly on the floor, and said, "I want to go out and forget everything."

Mark bobbed his head and said, "I'd feel the same way in your shoes. But I don't think that's such a good idea. You could be sick. Beer might make everything worse."

This was not what Michael wanted to hear. "I'm not sick! I just tripped, that's all. Come on, let's go to Fat Manny's."

Mark looked uncomfortable. "I don't want to go out tonight, man. With everything today, I just...I got a bad feeling. If you really want to drink, let's just stay here. We can watch TV and drink my dad's beer, he won't notice."

"Don't give me that bullshit," Michael said. "Mark, if I start living like I'm afraid of everything that might go wrong, I'm already beat. I've got to go out and do something, man."

"All right, fine, fine. But you need to clean up. You look like absolute crap, man."

Mark strummed some chords on the guitar while Michael splashed some water on his face in the bathroom. Mark wasn't the best guitarist in the world, but even Michael had to admit he knew how to play a decent repertoire of classic rock. From the bathroom, Michael commented that musicians were basically just servants to their audience.

"You're such a cynic," Mark said.

"They are. Just look at the money side of things. They have to play something other people like or they don't get paid."

"If they're good songwriters, people will like what they play. And what about taste? Don't you like listening to certain artists more than others?"

"Of course, I do!" Michael said. "That's why I pay for their music at all. So they can continue to entertain me."

"You don't think athletes have the same problem?" Mark said.

Michael just snorted.

This sort of tangent was why Mark didn't usually bring his guitar out when Michael was around, and he put his instrument away. It was obvious he liked playing, but Mark wasn't going to be the subject of Michael's ridicule. It was one of the things Michael liked about Mark. He had pride. No matter how much Michael needled him about things—like having a crap job, or not running as fast as he did—Mark stood on his own two feet. He had real pride about what he did and wouldn't let anyone take that away from him, not even his best friend. At times, Michael almost admired Mark for this, though of course he didn't want to be like him.

Michael emerged from the bathroom. Mark whistled and said, "Dang, you clean up well." Indeed, while Michael's injuries were still clearly visible, removing the grime had returned a freshness to him as though he had just stepped out of the shower. Each strand of hair lay meticulously in place.

Michael nodded and winked. "Let's go."

"Give me a minute." Not to be outdone, Mark took a few minutes to change and comb his hair. "All right. Let's roll."

They took the back roads to reach Fat Manny's Cantina, a small bar located in one of the tiny old Mexican villages in the valley south of Las Cruces. The road took them past the valley's huge pecan or-chards, long rows of ghostly trees perfectly aligned like identical tombstones in a vast cemetery. The moon's reflection glimmered eerily in the puddles of irrigation water and between the branches of the trees, as though it were bounding through the trees beside them. The cool evening wind blew leaves across the road. Michael shuddered; they looked like thousands of insects scuttling around in the baleful light. He began to feel more than a little of that bad feeling Mark had mentioned earlier. Maybe it was a mistake to go out after all. But what was he going to do? Tell Mark he'd been right and turn around? No chance.

Outside the cantina, they could hear the jukebox playing a song from The Doors. It was the kind of place that never played any new music, and the patrons liked it that way. Though they had been there before, both Michael and Mark felt out of place when they stepped inside. No one actually turned to look at them, but the atmosphere of the bar seemed to shift as they entered, the way it does when a

JOURNEY OF THE SPIRIT MAN

principal walks into a classroom in the middle of a teacher's lesson. Michael and Mark looked around for a place to sit, trying to shake off the strange feeling, and felt lucky to find two seats in a corner of the room.

"I'll buy the first round," Michael said. He planned to get good and drunk. See if anything as silly as a race or a girl bothered him once he had some booze in his gut.

"You get what you want," Mark told him, "I don't want to drink tonight."

"Come on, man. We didn't drive all the way out here to drink a Shirley Temple."

Michael ordered a pitcher of beer and two shots of tequila, shrugging when Mark refused to drink, and tossed back both shots in quick order, sucking the juice from a chunk of lime. He poured two mugs full of beer, drinking the foam off the top of one of them, then sat back and cast a watchful eye over the room. Four men were playing at the pool table in the center of the bar.

Michael sipped his beer and watched the men for a few moments, then said, "I can beat them, Mark." Pool was just another thing that came easily to him. He had inherited the passion for it from his father, who kept a pool table in the den. The two of them had spent many nights playing pool together when he was younger, although not so much recently.

"I'm sure you can," Mark said, "but they look like they want to be left alone."

"Is that right?" Michael said.

"You better not get us in trouble."

"Would you lighten up?" Michael slicked his hair back with his hands and stood. "I'll just hustle a couple of bucks and then we'll leave."

"Those guys don't look like the type you should hustle," Mark warned. "Let's just drink our beer and get the hell out of here, okay?"

But Michael had already sauntered over and put two quarters down on the table.

When the previous game was over, the winner glanced around

the bar to see who had put up the quarters.

Michael nodded at him. "What's up?" he said. He picked up a stick, looked down its length and then selected another. "What are we playing?"

"It's gonna cost you five to find out." He was a few years older than Michael, with various tattoos covering his arms. His face was clean-shaven, and he wore his long hair in a ponytail that came down past his shoulder. He powdered his stick and waited for an answer.

"No problem," Michael said. He pulled a thick wad of bills from his pocket, searched around for a five, and smoothed it on the edge of the table. "Let's do it."

"8-ball. Call the bank. No slop."

The man shot first, breaking the balls widely with a crack, sinking two solids.

Michael positioned himself, shot, and missed.

The man could barely contain his smile and walked around to the other side of the pool table. He shot again and made four before he missed.

Michael grabbed his pool stick and scratched. The men in the bar watching laughed and Michael swung his pool stick around.

"Man, I thought I had that one cold," he said.

Ponytail snorted, took up his cue to shoot again, and quickly finished the game. Michael handed the five dollars over and turned to leave the pool table when the man stopped him. "You can stay in, college boy, but it costs ten dollars."

"Oh, the big money now, huh? Okay, I'll try it one more time." He placed a ten on the table, racked up the balls, and stopped by Mark's table for a swig of beer.

"Michael, seriously, don't try to hustle these guys. Let's just leave," Mark said.

"Seriously," Michael mocked. "Have another beer, man. This isn't going to take long."

The second game followed the same pattern as the first. Michael played the same swaggering role, except that the tequila was beginning to show, and he was even more furious at himself when he lost. "Dammit," he swore. "I need another tequila to get focused. Another ten?"

"It'll cost you fifty bucks to stay in the game this time," the man said.

"Fifty bucks?" Michael said. "That's a lot of money."

Ponytail taunted him, "Come on, rich boy. You just had a bad run. You're not afraid, are you?"

"No," Michael said. "I'm not afraid." He put a fifty on the table, and then rolled his stick on the pool table to check if it was straight. "I'll play fifty if you let me break."

Ponytail agreed, eyes only on Michael's money, and the balls were quickly racked.

On Michael's break, he sank two stripes in the corner pockets. "Oh wow!" he cheered, as though he had never done that before. He lined up an inferior shot before he changed his mind and set up another. The target ball dropped and the cue rolled smoothly to set up a great shot in front of another. "Hey, it's a duck, but we take what we get, right?" he said as he dunked it with a crisp click. He positioned each ball perfectly and never missed a single shot. "Wow! My first perfect game!"

"You think you're slick, don't you?" Ponytail said as he tossed a fifty at Michael.

"Just working my way through college," Michael said. He plucked the money from the table and walked back to the corner where Mark sat nervously watching the disgruntled group of players.

"Are you happy now?" Mark asked. "Let's get out of here."

When they got outside, the wind was blowing in chilly gusts that cut right through their clothes. The sky was almost clear, except for a few high wind-tattered cirrus clouds, glowing in the moonlight, clawing at the moon with ghostly fingers.

"I can't believe what you just did," Mark said.

"At least something went right for me today," Michael said.

They reached the car but a man Michael didn't recognize was waiting for them. He pulled out a knife.

"I'll take all the money you just hustled...plus whatever else you have on you."

"Are you kidding me?" Michael said.

The assailant lunged forward, knifepoint swiping Michael's chin, drawing a thin line of blood. Nose to nose, they stared into each other's eyes. Something flashed in the man's eyes, something familiar, and just for a second, he looked haggard and bloody like he had been beaten. Michael saw, inexplicably, silver chains slung around his body, chaining him to a splintered wooden cross. There was a strange roaring in Michael's ears, like a crowd yelling and screaming, but for what he couldn't tell. Michael's view of the man wavered, like a mirage of water on the road on a hot day, and he saw Mark being dragged out into an arena. Crowds of people screamed and chanted words that Michael couldn't understand. They began throwing things. Mark staggered and fell, his body bruised and bloody.

"Do I look like I'm kidding?" the man asked. The noise stopped and now the mugger looked once again like nothing more than an unstable man who had spent too much time in bars and around the wrong sorts of people. Mark stood upright and unbloodied. What the hell was happening? Was Michael losing it?

It didn't matter. What mattered was that the guy with the knife was clearly running out of patience. As the reality of the situation reasserted itself, Michael felt fear wrap itself around his throat. This could go really, really wrong.

"Okay, okay," Michael whispered, slowly reaching into his pocket and pulling out his cash. "Here. Have it."

The man snatched it away and sneered. "Oh, you think you're so much better than me, don't you? 'Here. Have it,'" he mimicked in a high voice. "As if you're doing me a *favor*." His eyes swiveled down to Michael's hand. "I'll take that ring, too."

Panic swelled in Michael's chest. Not that. "Look, man, you already have all my money," Michael said. He felt like he was treading a thin line between reasoning and begging. But the last thing he wanted was to give up his lucky ring. Didn't he need it now more than ever?

"Wrong answer!" The man leapt forward, ready to thrust the knife into Michael's neck, but Mark intercepted him with an explosive cry and tried to grab the man's arm. He missed.

Everything happened quickly after that. The man thrust his knife into Mark's stomach once, twice, three times, then disappeared into the darkness even as Mark fell backwards into Michael.

"Oh, God," Mark said softly, and collapsed.

"Oh, Jesus," Michael cried. A sticky, dark circle expanded rapidly across Mark's shirt and when he tried to speak nothing but a gush of blood came out. Michael tried to put pressure on the wound, the only thing he could remember he was supposed to do in situations like this. Mark's blood covered his hands and soon began to pool on the ground beneath him. Michael choked and gagged and looked around at the lonely night, the lonely parking lot empty of anyone but him and Mark.

"Help!" he cried. "Somebody call an ambulance! Help him!"

His cries drew a small crowd out of the bar, people who formed a ring around the scene but kept their distance. Someone called 911. Everybody gathered around and stared. Michael sat beside Mark, covered in his blood.

Nothing felt real.

"Mark," he said. "Mark."

Mark's eyes met Michael's and he moved his lips as if to speak but made no sound. A trickle of blood spilled out. Then his lips stopped moving and his eyes stopped moving and even before checking for a pulse Michael knew that his best friend was dead. He went through the motions of checking Mark's wrist and leaning in close to feel for breath, but he already knew.

It took twenty minutes for the ambulance to arrive. A swarm of cops beat them by ten.

A stocky middle-aged man, wearing a trench coat over a brown suit, surveyed the scene for a minute, looking over a page in a small notebook. Finally, he approached Michael.

"My name is Detective Hinojosa," he said. "I'm leading the investigation into your friend's murder. I'm here to help you."

There was something about the detective's deep voice that Michael found reassuring. Still, he could only lean against the patrol car, unable to say anything, his mind mercifully numb.

"We're going to get this guy, if you help us," said the detective. "I need you to try and think as clearly as you can about what happened. I need to know what the guy looked like and who else might have been around. Focus on the facts. You don't want to let him get away with this, right?"

Michael blinked, forcing himself to focus, forcing words to leave his throat. "No. No, I don't," he said. He described the stranger who killed Mark as best as he could, but even as he pieced together his description he found himself doubting it. The man had been short, right? Had his hair been dark or did it just look that way in the unlit parking lot? When he tried harder to recall the details, the only image which kept coming back to him was the arena, the cross, the silver chains.

The detective recorded everything Michael said in his notepad despite Michael's uncertainty. When Michael had finally finished, the detective scribbled down a few last notes and asked, "Have you been drinking tonight? Can you drive down to the station?"

"Well, I...uh..."

"Never mind. Give me your keys." He held out his hand while Michael fished them out of his pocket. "Charlie!" he yelled at one of the officers. The officer jogged over. "Take Michael to the station. We need to get his deposition."

An hour later, Michael sat on an uncomfortable metal chair at the police station, waiting for the detective to return with more questions. He stared blankly at an ancient D.A.R.E. Poster on the wall across from him, wondering vaguely if they'd ever put up something new. He felt adrift on a sea with no land in sight, and with each slow-passing minute it seemed more and more certain that land would never appear. If this was real....No. He'd sooner believe the strange mirages he saw on the track were real.

"Michael. Michael!"

Michael looked up, realizing the detective had returned and was standing right in front of him, trying to get his attention.

"We found a man hitchhiking on the Old Mesilla Highway. Can you come tell us if you saw him earlier tonight?"

It took a moment for the words to register and the only thing that came out of his mouth was, "What?"

The detective repeated himself patiently and Michael felt a surge of adrenaline, hot rage fueling him with a sudden purpose and energy.

"Let me see him," he said.

The detective took him to a small interrogation room, where two officers stood next to a man whose hands were cuffed to the table in front of him. When Michael saw the man's eyes, his flesh went cold. It was him. The killer.

The man averted his eyes as if that would stop Michael from recognizing him.

Detective Hinojosa watched Michael carefully. "Do you recognize this man, Michael?" he said, as though the man wasn't in the room.

"You bastard," Michael cried. "I'll kill you!" He lunged at the killer but the cops were quick to block his way and hold him back.

"Come here and try it, rich boy," the killer said. He spat at Michael.

Michael felt himself dragged out into the hall. He collapsed into a chair and held his face in his hands, shaking, weeping. When he calmed down a bit, he shuddered and looked over at the detective.

"I swear, if you let him out, I will kill him." Michael said.

"Michael, go home to your family," the detective said. "Go get some sleep. There is nothing you can do. We'll call you in the morning."

"What about Mark's family? Who'll tell them? What are they going to tell them?" Michael's voice choked up and tears burned his eyes once again.

"It's being taken care of," the detective said. "Don't you worry about it." He placed a reassuring hand on Michael's shoulder. "We'll handle everything else that's left to be done."

Michael staggered outside into the night. One of the cops had brought his Hummer to the station. He got in and drove.

The wind blew hard and relentless. Street lamps cast a rusty glow along streets filled with whirling dust and trash. The wind pushed the car from side to side, the headlight beams shuddering back and forth across the street. Michael felt his rage building with the growing storm. That bastard. That murderer. If only they hadn't gone to that bar...if only Michael hadn't flashed his cash at that damn pool table...Michael screamed in rage and smashed his fist into the dashboard until it started to bleed.

At his house, his anger abandoned him, leaving a deep black well of nothingness in its wake. He stood in the dark parlor for a long time, utterly alone but for the ticking clock on the wall. When he couldn't take it any longer, he walked up the stairs to his parents' bedroom and tapped on the door. When at first no one answered he realized he had no idea how late it was. Irrational fear flooded him at the thought that his parents might not answer the door at all, might never answer the door, and he tapped again.

When his mother opened the bedroom door, clutching her robe and looking concerned, he fell into her arms and bawled. When at last he was able to push out some strangled words he said, "Mom... Mark's dead."

"What?" His father jumped up and turned the bedside lamp on.

Michael could only imagine how awful he must have looked. His hair was tangled, his eyes a hot red, his face pale. It reflected the horror he felt inside.

"Someone stabbed Mark," he said and leaned back against his mother, weeping.

She led him to the bed and held him and rocked him as he wept. "What happened?"

"It was all my fault." Michael wasn't sure he believed it—he *couldn't* believe it—but he wanted somebody, his parents, Mark's parents, the police, or anyone, to tell him outright that it wasn't his fault at all. He wanted somebody to tell him he couldn't have possibly known.

"I took him out to go drinking and got him killed," he said.

"What the hell happened?" his father said.

Michael tried and failed to keep his voice steady as he spoke. "I

JOURNEY OF THE SPIRIT MAN

hustled some guys playing pool. I just—" He couldn't say the words out loud but he knew the truth the moment he thought them: *I just wanted to win something.* "When we left, we got jumped. I gave this guy all my money but when he went to take my ring....He tried to stab me. Mark stopped him and—and—" Michael's voice cracked and he put his face in his hands.

Tears sprang to his mother's eyes as her grip on Michael tightened. He let her hold him, wishing he could forget everything and be a little boy again. If he was just a kid, this would never have happened. He could go back in time, to before college, before high school, before even middle school—to when he first met Mark and they used to ride their bikes together to the park to play baseball.

"Did you go to the police?" his father said.

"They already got the guy who did it." He wished he felt more satisfaction at this fact, but the truth was, knowing Mark's killer was behind bars did very little to quell his anger and the ache which throbbed beneath it. The anger told him if he could just get his hands around the killer's neck, he'd feel better. The ache told him he would never feel better.

They sat in silence for a long time, Michael working hard to hold back more tears. Finally, he stood. "I guess I should go to bed," he said.

His father hugged him tight. "If you're sure. If you need anything, just holler."

As Michael closed the door, he could hear the soft murmur of their voices, the rustling of the sheets. It would take them a long time to fall back asleep. He was pretty sure he wouldn't be able to sleep at all.

He stumbled upstairs, locked the door, and fell onto his bed. He checked his phone for messages but found none. Not even from Wendy. He sent her a brief text message. *Mark was stabbed tonight. He died. Can you call me?*

He wasn't proud of the text, but maybe she would pity him and text back. Or call.

She didn't.

He wished he'd tacked on the word "please" to his request. Perhaps even an "I love you," "I miss you," or "I need you." But, as before, he simply wasn't able to admit any of these things.

Well, screw her. There were other women out there, women who would call him back. He'd text them next—when he didn't feel so bad. His head rang like a man beaten hard, and the room reeled. His sides aching from sobbing. A wave of nausea swept over him all at once and he reached for the trash can under his desk just in time. His stomach already empty, nothing came out but a yellow strand of bile. The nausea subsided but he found himself unable to move, unable to summon the strength required to lift himself away from the garbage pail and the droplet of bile at its base. Instead he sank the rest of the way to the floor and stared at the carpet and the doorway and the dark house beyond. He watched the night's stillness and waited for something to happen, for the credits to roll and the lights to come back on and for Mark to punch him in the shoulder as they stood and make some stupid joke about what a wild movie they'd just seen. But none of this happened. The movie did not end. The night and its silence stretched on and on into eternity.

Chapter 4

The days blurred by in a whirlwind of alternating blankness and despair.

Michael's doctor prescribed sedatives to help him fall asleep, but he slept only fitfully, and found himself startled awake, sweating, panting, hand to his heart, trying to catch his breath after having the same dream, the same nightmare, night after night after night. He could never remember what took place in these nightmares— only the panic which pervaded them. Most days, Michael barely left his room. He put his phone on silent and let the battery run down to nothing. He kept the heavy drapes closed and lay under heavy blankets and let the thick silence envelop him as he sank to the ocean floor. He wanted to expel every molecule of air from his lungs, to just breathe in the sad silence, to dive in it, to drown in it.

His mother knocked on the door each day like clockwork: at 7 a.m. before she left for work and at 8 p.m. when she returned. In the mornings she left food by his door, and in the evenings, more often than not, she found the food uneaten.

"We'll let him mourn for a week," Michael heard his mother whisper one morning. Like they could control his pain, turn it off like a tap.

In his half-awake state he wondered how long it took to starve to death. He recognized the thought as a childish one, an absurd idea, but it carried a certain appeal nonetheless; just shrinking down and down and down until he became nothing.

When Michael finally plugged his phone in and booted it up, he saw a text from Wendy. The momentary jolt of lightness at her name quickly dissipated. The message was brief and simple. *I'm really sorry. I know how much Mark meant to you.*

Michael threw his phone against the wall and retreated under the covers once more. Later, when he went to pick it up, it wouldn't turn on at all. He really did break everything he touched.

He skipped his doctor's appointment, scheduled three days before Mark's funeral. It all seemed so trivial now and he just couldn't face it. They'd tell him what was wrong. Maybe it was nothing. Probably it was nothing. They'd tell him he had simply tripped and his loss wasn't the result of any mysterious ailment but his own fault entirely. They'd tell him maybe he just wasn't as strong as he thought he was. But he'd already started to figure this out, so what was the point in showing up?

His doctor, however, wouldn't leave him alone. When Michael didn't show up for the appointment or answer his cell, the doctor called his home phone. Michael answered, thinking maybe it was his mom, calling from the hospital. He almost hung up when he heard the voice on the other end.

"Michael, it's Dr. Saniscoy."

"Oh, hello." He sounded like a sullen little kid. He was a sullen little kid. He definitely didn't have the energy for this right now.

"You missed your appointment," Dr. Saniscoy said.

"I know." He didn't explain, didn't apologize. Who cared anymore?

"We got your test results. Can you answer a few questions to confirm your identity?"

Michael did so grudgingly. Better than going to the hospital again.

With that, the doctor launched into a long, rambling monologue which, after a while, barely sounded like words anymore. All the syllables merged together to form an incomprehensible band of white noise. Michael was able to pick out enough words to get the picture. Chronic. Degenerative. Incurable.

He interrupted the doctor's speech. "Am I dying?"

"Not...exactly. The disease moves differently in everyone, and it moves at different speeds. But no, I wouldn't say you're dying at all."

"Will I be able to run?"

There was a long pause at the other end of the line. "For a while, yes."

"How long?"

"It's hard to say. Like I said, the disease progression isn't linear and the rate isn't fixed. You might barely even notice you're sick for the next ten years, even the next twenty. After that...well, we'll worry about that when we get there. What's most important right now is that we keep a close eye on..."

The doctor's voice blurred back into white noise, indecipherable sounds. Michael was somewhere far, far away. Running on a mountaintop. Running away. That was all he wanted. Just to get away from everybody and everything. If he was fast enough, maybe he could even outrun everything the doctor was telling him. He hung up while the doctor was still speaking. When he went back upstairs and lay on his bed, he had the strange sensation that he was not alone. The mirages from his childhood seemed to dance at the corners of his vision and in the dark corners of his room. Were they taunting him? Or were they urging him forward?

Michael forced himself out of bed three days later, the morning of Mark's funeral. He turned on the lights for the first time in days and they pierced straight through his skull. He winced and covered his eyes with his palms.

He combed his hair and knotted his tie as best he could, though his fingers felt thick and clumsy with fatigue. He stared at the haggard, red-eyed face in the mirror for a long time, uncertain of who he was looking at. He recalled an old cliché about "grief beyond tears" and wished he could find that place, instead of breaking down again and again at random times throughout the day. He was tired of crying. He was tired of having an ache in his chest that made it hard to breathe. He was tired of everything.

Would Wendy even recognize him now? Would she feel pity? It didn't matter. If he was Wendy, he certainly would have moved on by now. She wouldn't want to share the burden of his illness. His growing illness. And good for her. She'd marry some rich, handsome man—the man Michael had thought he was destined to become.

His father knocked and Michael emerged, steeling himself to step out into the world once again. As the two of them walked down the stairs, Michael felt the urge to tell his father about the test results. He was a doctor, after all, and he might know something. He might be able to offer a second, less dire opinion. Or he could call in some favors and ensure Michael received top of the line treatment someplace like Mayo Clinic.

But something stopped the words before he could form them. He couldn't help but think of himself 500 years from now, decrepit and immobile but kept alive by wires and tubes and beeping machinery. The ever-aging immortal, a real life Tithonus. The medical community would keep him in the finest medical university of the 26th century, checking his vitals in the morning and wheeling him out to the lobby for people to see "Michael Seymour: Wonder of the Human Race." Tourists would pose for pictures beside his fragile body. Teens would doodle on him with felt tip markers. He would only be able to sit and stare. Even his breathing, by then, would be conducted by machines.

No. The disease would run its course. He wouldn't become a human lab rat.

Michael's mother met them in the foyer. She was dressed all in black for the ceremony and Michael was surprised to see tears running down her cheeks. She had liked Mark, but until now, she had been strong and consoling and had not wept at all—at least not in front of him.

Michael's father moved to put his arm around her shoulder but she waved him off. "Mark's mother just called," she said. "She... she asked us not to come. She asked us not to go to the funeral. Michael, I'm so sorry, baby."

The words struck Michael with the same breath-stopping shock as jumping into ice water on a sunny day. He didn't know what to say or what to do with his arms hanging useless at his sides. For the past week, he had been wracked with fear that everybody would blame him for Mark's death. Well, now he knew. They did. At least, Mark's parents did.

Michael wanted to hit something. He wanted to break something and hear it shatter, see the shards of glass scattering and the bright red streaks blooming across his fist. But there was nothing here at which to aim his rage—only his parents, who stared at him as if he himself were on the verge of shattering.

Before he knew what he was doing, he pushed past his father and dashed for the door. His parents called after him but they couldn't stop him and soon their voices were swallowed up by the rush of wind around his ears. He ran. And ran. Away from the house and down the path that led into the desert and towards the mountains. He ran until his sides hurt, until his vision lost its color, until his spit was so thick he couldn't spit at all, and he prayed he could somehow run himself into oblivion. Pain built in his legs but the burning only fueled his determination to run faster and harder.

The mountains rose higher and higher as he approached. The slope steepened as he drove himself onward. He had climbed these mountains a hundred times before and hurled himself up the rocks without pausing. He rounded a bend where the path grew narrow and beyond the lip a sheer cliff waited, and as he did so something caught his eye. There, on the dead branch of a petrified tree, perched a vulture. It wasn't an uncommon sight, but this one seemed to be looking directly at him, and he was struck by a strange, inexplicable thought. *It's a death omen. It's here for me.*

Then he slipped.

Michael tried to grab onto something to stop his fall but found nothing but loose rocks beneath his fingers as his body pitched over the precipice. He didn't even have time to scream before his head collided with a boulder and a ball of light exploded in the back of his head and he finally found the nothingness he had been seeking.

When he woke up, Michael found himself halfway propped against a rock face and apparently having lost the entire day. The desert glowed a deep orange and long shadows stretched across its length. Michael tried to move and a wave of nausea ran through him. He ached all over, but, miraculously, nothing seemed to be broken. He touched two fingers to the back of his head and they came away dark with blood. Moving more slowly this time, he managed to stand up with minimal nausea. That's when he saw it.

On the mountainside not forty feet away stood an ancient adobe gate. It was heavy, thick and deeply carved with strange designs he couldn't quite make out from a distance. Massive wrought-iron hinges fastened the doors to two huge iron pillars, but there was nothing beyond these in either direction—no wall of any sort. The gate appeared to have been weathered by centuries, but Michael was absolutely certain he had never seen it there before. He had run the surrounding mountain trails since he was in middle school and never before had he seen such a gate. He stepped towards it, cautious and limping, discovering new injuries along the way. When he finally reached it, he raised the hand-wrought latch and gave the door a push. It creaked, but swung smoothly open.

Through the gate was only the other side of the mountain path. Michael laughed. What else had he expected to find? He felt silly that he had, for even a single moment, let himself believe something different waited on the other side. With a bit of his old bravado, he took three swaggering steps through the door, pretending to be royalty in some faraway land. When he turned and looked back, however, his confidence vanished. The door was gone. Had it ever been there in the first place? Or were his childish mirages returning thanks to what was almost certainly a severe concussion?

When he turned again, this time in the direction that should have led home, those questions were dispelled by new, much different questions. Because the landscape no longer bore any resemblance at all to the mountain path he knew so well.

He was standing on a small hill in a desert; a desolate, waterless land, strange and unreal. The sky was a blaze of flashing colors, in swirling motion as though hurtling through a rush of atmospheric mood swings. The sun was not a warm gold but a crystalline blue-white. The wind, as if painted, was visible in the air as feathered currents of canary yellow, lime green, dark blue, and maroon.

Michael looked around to see if he might spot the gate again, but he couldn't find it. In all directions, he could only see rolling hills and dunes, with nothing around that could give him a reference point. Whenever he looked back at a place, he had the uncanny feeling that the hills had moved, like slow swells in a sea of sand.

Michael had been lost before, but never like this. He had no idea how to even begin searching for a way back. Then again, what was waiting for him back in Las Cruces anyway? A romantic relationship? Not since he ruined it. A best friend? Not since he got him killed. A future as a star athlete? Get real. Everything he'd thought was a sure thing had slipped from his grasp in a matter of days and now even his home had escaped him. He wanted to shout at the sky and ask why. He wanted the demand the universe tell him why he, of all people, deserved this. But his throat was too parched and he knew the sky wouldn't answer anyway.

Whatever. He would do what he always had and rely on himself. He could find his way out of whatever strange place he'd crash-landed into.

Before setting out, Michael took his tie off and buried it halfway in the sand to act as a marker. Then he stood and started walking towards the setting sun. The strange thing, he realized, was that the sun should have been obscured by the mountains if he had, as he suspected, fallen on the opposite side of the range. But there was nothing on the horizon besides low dunes. Where the hell was he, and how had he ended up here?

With only the trail and the sunset to guide him, Michael walked toward the fading light.

Chapter 5

After a while, the narrow trail he was following developed into a wider footpath. Probably a good sign. He hoped he'd run into someone sooner rather than later. Maybe an evening jogger who could point the way back home. But the dunes rolled like an endless red ocean across the horizon and nowhere on any of them did he see any other living things. A harsh wind kicked up and blew sand into Michael's eyes, into his ears, and down the collar of his dirty white dress shirt. The sand felt like needles against his scrapes and bruises. Despite the wind and the shifting dunes, however, the footpath remained curiously intact, as though the shifting flow of the sand deliberately avoided this winding route.

Shadows played in the canyons and valleys as the brilliant colors in the swirling sky changed from crimson and chartreuse to purple and a deep murky green. The temperature was dropping quickly. Though it felt heavenly to get a break from the searing heat, Michael knew all too well that a bitter cold would follow. He'd have to keep walking no matter what.

Darkness came. A kaleidoscope of stars moved in rhythmic geometric patterns and lit up the sky. Shifting bands of color wove through them, a pulsing nebula extending out into the depths of space as though to embrace the brilliant arc-light jewels of the stars above. Michael had never seen the northern lights before, but he imagined they couldn't be any more beautiful than the display unfurling above him in this moment. For a while, he almost didn't mind how alien everything felt.

The temperature dropped. Michael's mouth was as dry as wasteland around him and thoughts of cool, clear water were growing harder and harder to keep at bay. His feet ached and he had destroyed his dress shoes walking through the sand and running

JOURNEY OF THE SPIRIT MAN

along the rocks. How many miles had he traveled so far? How many miles was he from the adobe gate? How long had he been walking, anyway? And besides all that, what the hell was this place? Was it any place at all? He shook his head and wished he had his good running shoes.

Michael's feet were developing nasty rashes and blisters from the sand that had accumulated in his shoes. He stopped and turned over one of his shoes to dump out the unmerciful particles of agate, silicon, and just plain meanness. A small steady stream of grit began to flow from the toes of the shoe, rolling down the tongue and out into the open air to be caught by the wind, blown miles and miles across the barren wilderness. More sand came out of the shoe with another shake and then more and more.

Michael stared, watching a now continuous fountain of sand flowing from his shoe, as though the entire desert was contained within. The wind laughed as it caught every particle and carried them this way and that. Michael finally turned the shoe over to look inside. It looked as though he had pulled it from his closet after months of disuse. There were bits of dust inside, but nothing more. He must really be dehydrated if he was hallucinating this badly.

He felt around the inside of the shoe. The sole was paper thin. He was afraid to push it very hard; his finger might just poke through. No sand. He slipped on his shoes, which still felt as though they were full of sand, and resumed his long walk.

As he walked, he imagined the blowing sand slowly carving away at his body, like eroding a statue. If he fell, he feared the sand would simply drain away what little water remained in his body and his bones would crumble into dust and nothing would be left of him for anyone to find.

This thought brought with it the sudden fear that he would die alone in this unknown place. Die and never be able to say goodbye to his parents. Or Wendy. Now that Mark was gone, he didn't really have anyone else to say goodbye to. Despite all of his boasting to Mark, nobody else really mattered. Or, if he was honest, cared.

Another unsettling idea occurred to him as he looked across the vast, peculiar sky. He put his hand to his head and it was still sore to the touch. Had he been killed in the fall? Was this his life after death? Although the landscape was alien, the trail and the dunes seemed as real as anything he had ever known. The sand was real when he kicked it, and so were the outcroppings of rock. If he could still feel the ground, his feet, his thirst, then surely he couldn't be dead, could he?

His musings were interrupted by the sudden appearance of strange vegetation blocking his path. It was a rich, dark wall of shrubs overflowing with broad leaves, so many that he couldn't see the stem or the ground beneath it. When he tried to move a branch aside, he jumped back in pain. Thick, dark thorns, coarse and vicious, stuck to his palm like hooks.

Michael sat down on a rock, closed his eyes, and pulled out the barbed thorns one by one by one. If this place truly was death, then he had just made the unfortunate discovery that death was not free from pain. Quite the opposite, in fact—the thorns had stung more than anything as he extracted them from his hand.

Okay, so moving the shrub aside wasn't going to work. The wall stretched on and on in both directions as far as he could see, so he picked a direction—left—and started walking. It had to end eventually, and then he'd find his way back to the path. His strides grew heavier. He wanted nothing more than to lie down and fall asleep. Had there been poison in those thorns?

He shook his head. He had to keep going. He had to stay awake. And he had to find water. That took priority over just about everything else. If he didn't find his way home and didn't find water, his chances of surviving tomorrow's searing sun were roughly zero.

As though the desert had read his mind, a pond appeared in front of him. The baleful firefly green light of the night sky reflected perfectly from its still surface. As he approached, he noted more dark, needle-bearing shrubbery surrounding it. But he had to have water. It took a long time, at least the better part of an hour, to carefully pick his way through the shrubs to reach the water, but he managed it with only a few pricks here and there.

He fell to his knees at the shore, thirsty beyond anything he had ever experienced before, and reached out his hands to scoop up some water—then recoiled from the fetid stench that stung his nose. Moss and slime swam on the surface of the stagnant puddle and bubbles belched to release a dark green swamp gas.

Despite all this, he knew he would die if he didn't drink anything. He cleared a patch of debris, filled his hands, and forced himself to drink. The water made him gag, but he forced it down, then immediately regretted it. His body rebelled, retching and expelling the water in forceful projectiles from both his mouth and nose.

He stood, still queasy, and wiped his mouth with his sleeve. He should've known better than to try drinking that foul stuff. A stupid mistake. He surveyed his surroundings in the murky half-light and noticed something he hadn't spotted initially: footprints. They led away from the water and up the nearest hillside.

Michael picked his way through the shrubs again, earning himself a few more pricks and scratches, then followed the footprints. Whoever they belonged to must have come through here recently, or else the wind would have wiped away any trace of their passage. If he could catch up to them, he could ask for help getting home. When he crested the next dune, he was astonished to discover a city in the distance. The walls appeared to be high mud-brick walls, like an ancient pueblo. His relief at the sight was immediately tempered by what encircled it. Like the pond, the city was situated inside walls of thick thorn bushes, surrounded completely by a forest of the tangled limbs.

Michael didn't remember anything like this anywhere around Las Cruces, and wondered once again where the hell he was. He didn't like the thought of pushing through all those thorns, but he looked back the way he had come and the thought of backtracking now seemed even worse. Once he made it to the city, everything would be all right. Even if he couldn't find someone willing to take him home tonight, maybe there would be a motel or something willing to put him up for the night, or a phone he could use to call his parents.

A falling star streaked across the dark sky and he wished for home.

What were his parents doing right now? Were they searching for him, worried? Or were they at home, relieved that he—and his anger and sadness—were gone for at least a little while? And Wendy, was she out with friends? What was she talking about, thinking about? Out here in this alien place, cut off from everyone and everything he knew, Michael found himself longing for all the things he had barely given a second thought before. Too late, of course. Far too late.

The cold was really setting in now. Michael's limbs were growing stiff and the thought of trying to pick a path through the thorns in this state didn't strike him as particularly wise. Better to wait for morning. With his hands he dug a hole in the sand just big enough to lay in a fetal position so he could sleep with some likeness to warmth. He lay down, wrapped his arms around his knees, and hoped he could get just a little warmer, warm enough to fall asleep. As sleep reached out toward him, he prayed he would dream of home.

Chapter 6

Michael awoke to the sound of neighing horses. A cloud of dust approached from the distance and at its head galloped a group of riders on horseback. It was still dark, but something about the riders sent a jolt of fear through Michael and he scrambled beneath the only cover he could find: a nearby tangle of thorny brush. The thorns raked his arms and his back and lodged in his skin but he managed to squirm under the shrub and out of sight.

Through the brambles, Michael watched the riders circle the indentation where he had slept. One of them dismounted, knelt, and caressed the sand. He motioned for the others to join him. All of them wore dented, filthy metal armor reminiscent of that worn by conquistadors. Long, rusted swords hung at their hips. The first rider noticed the tracks leading across the sand and looked directly at Michael in his hiding place.

"Shit," Michael said. He scrabbled away as fast as he could. Thorns tore at him, catching his clothes and skin. He emerged from the bramble, leapt to his feet, and started running. He might have nowhere to hide, but maybe his speed could save him.

"After him!" the rider shouted, unsheathing his sword.

Michael didn't make it very far. He staggered and fell onto the rough sand as a sudden pain shot through his leg. He kept going, crawling on all fours, but five horses quickly caught up and surrounded him, rearing and neighing, their riders laughing and hooting with a savage glee.

A net fell over him and that was the end of his flight. He rolled into a ball and waited to be stabbed or clubbed to death.

"Look at this," one of the riders said. "We will be rewarded handsomely for bringing this one."

The rider dismounted and approached Michael. He drew his

sword and putting its point against Michael's neck.

Michael cringed. "Please don't!"

The group of riders erupted in a rough laughter. The stench that wafted from them was horrific. A sickly sweet, decaying smell like that of rotting corpses. The leader pulled his sword back, then stomped and kicked Michael as the others dismounted. They removed the net and joined together to kick and beat him. Though they were obviously holding back to avoid killing him, they appeared to enjoy striking him hard enough to make him cry out.

"Stop! What did I do?"

The riders laughed even louder. One of them held Michael down, pressed a knee into his neck, and tied his hands behind his back.

"Take him to Gehenna!" the leader commanded the others. He then snatched Michael's ring right off his finger.

Michael tried to cry out in protest but the wind had been knocked out of him. His lucky ring was gone forever. Not that it had brought him much luck lately anyway. It was probably better that he lost it.

One of the riders tied a rope around Michael's neck and looped it around his horse's saddle horn. Everybody mounted their horses and began to ride, dragging Michael behind them through the sand. The rope chafed and choked him. Michael struggled to get up so he could run behind the horses.

He tried to speak, tried to reason with the riders or at least demand to know why or where they were taking him, but between the rope and his parched throat he could barely manage a faint rasp. Finally, he manage to force out a few words.

"I haven't done anything. I don't deserve to die."

"Of course you've done something," the chief rider said, "and everybody deserves to die."

As they approached the city, Michael finally got a good look at it. It was ringed with fire, dark ash-filled smoke spewed from crudely constructed cottages along its perimeter, but no matter how long they burned, none of the huts seemed at risk of collapsing. As they drew near, the heat scorched Michael's skin and made his eyes water. They dragged him across a red-hot iron drawbridge that melted what remained of his shoes. When his feet sank into those boiling soles, he couldn't help but scream. Blisters bubbled up and broke on the bottoms of his feet as they marched through the arched gate in the crumbling stone wall.

The city had elements of a once-great ancient civilization that had fallen into decay. There was little evidence of industrial technology, and people seemed to live in a kind of medieval peasant squalor. Smoke hung heavy in the air. The streets were wet, and the gutters and alleys brimmed with piles of human waste and garbage.

Great statues of warriors lay toppled over, their heads smashed to pieces on the ground beneath what remained of their feet. Water fountains, once masterful in their artistry, held shallow puddles of putrid sludge. Once-beautiful buildings, architectural wonders long ago, now lay in ruins, vandalized or burned to the ground.

The soldiers led him past the courtyard but the horrors did not end. In fact, they only grew worse with every painful step. The stench of decay became overpowering even before Michael saw the cause, and when he did he retched again, though this time nothing came out and the riders only laughed and pulled him forward. Countless bodies hung from the fortress walls, and dead men, women, and children lay in piles, covered in black-crusted blood. Swarms of flies buzzed into the air as the riders passed and maggots wriggled beneath the corpses' skin, eating their death.

Michael's tormentors dragged him down a dark alley where people scurried out of their way like rats, peering from dark corners with glowing eyes. One of them burst from the shadows and attacked a rider, trying to grab his reins in a desperate fury. But the soldier was quick. He swung his sword once, clipping cleanly through the man's neck. The man fell to the ground, gasping, a hideous gurgling sound coming from his throat as he drowned in his own blood.

They came to a larger square that seemed to be the center of the city and stopped, dismounted, and untied the rope around Michael's neck. They grabbed his arms and led roughly through a long corridor to a reeking chamber where only the light of two barely burning torches broke the all-encompassing darkness.

Screams echoed off the walls and stung Michael's ears. He breathed through his mouth to avoid the stench of the rotting bodies but it didn't help much; the scent lingered even on his tongue. Sweat poured down his forehead, and he trembled with shame when he couldn't keep urine from running down his leg. He grabbed onto the bars of a cell and retched again, horrified by the waves of weakness which swept over his body with each heave. The swamp water was having an obvious effect on him and his bowels emptied, soiling his pants and legs.

A man so thin that he looked like a skeleton, his grime-covered cheeks scabbed with pus and blood, pushed his face through the bars and hissed. His teeth were rotten and black.

"Maggot! You're dead, maggot!" His scream spewed dark phlegm that splattered against Michael's cheek. Another man growled at Michael, then stuck out his tongue and chewed it, grunting savagely, until a bloody pus-filled piece fell off. Michael's captors snatched him away from the cell and pulled him down the hallway to another cell and threw him inside. They slammed the door as Michael tumbled to the filthy stone. Behind him, he heard the key turn in the lock and his heart sank. No way out. He was going to die here.

"We'll be back for you later!" his captors called out, laughing. They made a lot of noise as they left, jeering at the inhabitants in the other cell.

The first thing that Michael noticed was the stench of urine. The second was something scampering along the floor, searching— for what? For food? Or for remains to feed on? He wished he had a flashlight. Or a torch. Even a single match would do. Anything to banish this darkness and whatever unknown horrors lurked within it. Although, on second thought, perhaps it was better to leave these horrors in the realm of the unknown, given what he had seen so far. The images from his trek through the city were burned into his brain as if with a white-hot brand. He knew if he somehow, someway escaped this wretched place, those images would never leave him.

He groped around in the dark, across the sticky floor, though for what he wasn't sure. The sounds of his movements echoed through the cell. He wanted to scream, he wanted to cry, he could not make himself utter a single sound.

Other sounds—shrieks and moans and howls of pain—were constant and came from near and far. Because of the way everything echoed, he couldn't tell where, exactly, any of the screams were coming from, which gave the impression they came from everywhere, all around him, all at once.

Michael's eyes couldn't adjust to the heavy darkness, but soon he sensed that someone else was in his cell. His hands were still tied behind his back and he wasn't sure if he would have the strength to fight even if the situation called for it. He pushed himself as far as he could into the corner of the cell.

Chains rattled as shadows revealed the silhouette of a man: Michael's mysterious cellmate stood up and moved across the floor towards him. He stopped just three feet away.

Michael sighed in relief when the man didn't come any closer. The chain must have prevented him from moving any farther, and there was no way that Michael would cross inside his range. For all he knew, the cell could be half a mile long, but he wasn't about to find out.

"What are you doing here?" the silhouette asked in a low voice.

Michael tried to speak, but couldn't.

"Hey! I'm talking to you. Can't you talk? Are you mute or something? You can certainly shit. I can smell it all over you. At least tell me what you did to get here."

"I don't know," Michael said. "I don't even know where 'here' is. Where am I?"

"You're in Gehenna. Your own personal Hell, exactly the way you want it to be, exactly what you think you deserve. So who are you and what did you do?"

"I don't know," Michael whimpered. Immediately, he felt ashamed. Was he a child who whined and whimpered when something bad happened? But he couldn't help it. He was afraid and alone and he desperately wanted to be anywhere else but here. He wanted to be back at his house, in his room with his mom and dad. He wasn't Michael Seymour, Champion Runner. He was Mikey, the six-year-old who had just crapped his pants and needed his mommy.

"It'll take you a long time to die," the silhouette said. "But that won't be the end. Oh no. After that you'll die and die and die and die, slowly each time, and soon you'll wish that—"

"Shut up!" The command came from outside the cell and both Michael and the silhouette turned towards the sound as the key turned in the lock and the door creaked open.

One of the riders entered and greeted Michael with a fist in the face. He grabbed Michael's collar and threw him out of the cell. Michael struggled to his feet and jumped out of the way, anticipating a kick to his backside. He successfully avoided it, but any satisfaction at this dodge was smacked off his face when a fist met him from behind. He staggered down the hallway in front of his captors. He glanced in the cells as he passed, each containing a progressively worse surprise. He passed a cell full of people smoking endlessly burning cigarettes and exhaling smoke from every hole and open wound in their body. Another cell contained two naked men fighting over a large ruby. They were emaciated, as though they hadn't stopped to eat for the last month.

One of the riders kicked him to make him pick up the pace.

They walked for miles. They passed another cell of men and women so tightly packed together that they lay on top of each other, forced into a grim, pleasureless orgy. Fake smiles were literally stapled to their faces and they groaned in agony. In the next cell, a shirtless man faced a wall, suspended by a rope tied around his waist, his feet barely touching the ground. A short man, standing only three and a half feet tall, held a whip, bloody from fresh beatings as well as old. He cracked the whip and shouted, "So you like beating on little kids? How do you like it when people beat on you?"

"I do-o-on't," the man blubbered.

Michael turned away, something deep inside of him sick and

growing sicker.

"Keep going!" said one of his escorts, pushing him forward.

In the next cell, two men beat each other mercilessly, continuing even when fingers and limbs fell off their bodies and both men slowly died from blood loss. Then their bones repaired themselves and their skin regenerated and they began the cycle again. A thief lying on the ground in another cell reached through the bars and snatched a chain off the armor of one of Michael's captors. Michael expected to see the man's hand get cut off and was surprised when he saw the rider laugh. The piece rose out of the thief's grasp into the air, as he waved madly trying to catch it. The chain floated up and into the cell a couple more feet and rested on a pile of treasure that piled on top of the thief, pinning him to the floor and slowly crushing him.

Michael shuddered. What would his fate be? What would his personal hell look like? Was this it? The endless walking through jail cells, watching other people be tortured in their own hells? They walked for hours into the depths of the dungeon. Michael lost track of the number of cells that they passed. The weight of the suffering he witnessed dragged behind him like a shroud.

Finally, a dull roar hummed along the hall and Michael felt the floor and walls vibrate with the low hum. The cavernous chill began to give way once more to heat, the humidity burning away entirely. A bright light in the distance bounced with each step. Soon, the heat was unbearable. Michael felt like he was walking into a furnace. The vibrating hum, that dull roar, was now a deafening pounding, like a hundred drummers drumming without meter or any sense of unity. It shook the walls.

The riders stopped in front of the light, which came through a small barred window. They threw Michael into the cell there, where three men cowered in the corners. The window let in a painful amount of light, illuminating the cell's squalor. Michael hesitated, afraid of what he might see, then looked outside. It was a huge colosseum, like Rome's greatest, and it seemed to be the only building in Gehenna not in a state of ruination. A series of gates on the same level as Michael's cell led to the arena and from behind them came a wave of curses and cheers. Thousands of spectators filled the stone seats above. A balcony projected out over the arena, where a judge and the jury sat. Another large gate stood on the flat side of the colosseum and rose to the height of the city wall. A huge cross stood in the center of the arena, chains swinging slowly from each end of the cross beam. Two guards dragged a man onto the field through the gate on the opposite side of the arena. They shackled him to the cross, striking and kicking him as he strained and pulled at the chains, trying to break free.

Then guards entered Michael's cell and seized one of the men. They took him into the arena and placed him before the judge and jury. The jurors spoke amongst themselves and to the two men in the arena, but Michael couldn't hear what they were saying. When they had apparently finished their deliberations, the jurors all sat back as though in silent expectation while the judge at the podium shouted some orders. One of the guards threw a large knife onto the sandy flood of the arena at the foot of the cross. The prisoner from Michael's cell walked to the knife and picked it up. He lifted the blade into the air and presented it to the crowd, as though in salute. The crowd went wild, cheering hoarsely in a deep-throated roar of approval. The prisoner circled the other man, taunting with the blade. The one chained to the cross thrashed wildly as the man with the knife lunged at him. Astonished, Michael watched the prisoner slash and mutilate his victim, starting out with small cuts and growing wilder with each thrust. When he could no longer raise the knife for another slice or thrust, he faced the judge and the crowd, who cheered. Somebody brought him a cape to put around his shoulders and led him to another gate on the ground level. He disappeared from sight.

The guards opened Michael's cell again. This time, they grabbed Michael by the arms and dragged him outside. He cringed as they neared the bloody cross, afraid he would be chained to it like the last victim, now being cut down. But instead, they led him to stand before the jury. The crowd cheered. The judge, a huge man dressed in black and wearing a tall pointed hat, signaled the crowd to be quiet. Michael could hear his own heartbeat, heavy and thudding in his ears.

"Michael," the judge called down. "It is time for your revenge. Behold."

The judge pointed toward the opposite gate, which swung open to reveal guards dragging another victim forward. The guards led him to the cross and clamped the shackles onto him. A strangled cry of rage and pain flew out from Michael's throat. He remembered this man. He knew this man. Michael had last seen him in the police interrogation room. Mark's killer.

"Kill him! Kill him!" the jury screamed. "He killed your friend."

Michael didn't pause to wonder how these people knew intimate details from his life. He didn't care. He looked at the killer and saw Mark's body, convulsing on the ground as he lay dying.

"Kill him! Kill him!" the jury shouted and the crowd took it up in a chant. "Kill him! Kill him!"

Anger rose up in Michael's throat, threatening to choke him. Now was his chance for revenge. The one thing that might save him from his grief, spare him from his nightmares. The crowd sensed his dark thoughts and they began to roar, bull-throated, a sound he could feel deep in his gut. Looking up, Michael caught a glimpse of the crowd's fists pounding the air, their mouths open as they howled for blood and death. For an instant, he thought he saw Wendy in the crowd, but she disappeared. The chants urged him on.

The judge threw him a sword. It swished through the air and thudded into the sand in front of the chained killer. Michael lunged. He screamed, holding it upright, ready to sink it deep into the killer's chest. The man hung loosely in the chains, babbling half incoherently, drooling, pleading for his life.

A quiet voice worked its way through the howls of the crowd and Michael's own bloodlust: "Don't do it. You're not a killer."

It was Mark's voice. But where was he? Then, out of the corner of his eye, Michael saw another prisoner being readied for the shackles. Shocked, he dropped the sword. The next victim was Mark.

"What's he doing here?" Michael said to the judge.

"What difference does it make? This is a place for revenge. Take yours and let others worry about the next prisoner."

Michael turned to look at Mark's killer. He was so small on that cross. So fragile. His body ruined, his mind shattered, just a shadow of a person who had once been someone's son.

"Kill him!" the crowd roared. "Kill him! Kill him! Kill him!"

But Mark's voice, though quiet, cut through all the noise.

"Don't do it, Michael. It won't fix anything. It won't bring me back."

Michael didn't understand, but he knew he had failed to listen to Mark once before and it had cost Mark his life. Now he took the sword in his hands and threw it as far away as he could. He held his hands up to the crowd, unbloodied.

"I won't do it," he shouted, his voice loud and clear, echoing around the colosseum.

The audience fell suddenly, shockingly silent.

The judge snatched his pointed hat and threw it on the ground. "What? *What?*"

The crowd leapt to its feet and roared as one, "Coward! Weakling! Appeaser!" They threw handfuls of trash at him. A banana peel hit his cheek and left a trail of slime.

"Get this abomination out of my sight," the judge said, ripping his cloak apart. Parts of the cloak that fluttered to the ground actually looked blue in a different light.

The ground beneath Michael trembled and lurched and he staggered to keep his balance. At the back of the colosseum, the huge gate creaked open, its sound cutting through the crowd's rumbling rage.

"Get out! Get out!" the crowd screamed, hurling animal dung and rotten fruit at him.

Michael had one thought in his mind: *Save Mark.* He scanned the arena, looking for something to break through the gate where Mark was trapped. But two guards grabbed Michael and began dragging him away. The third guard walked up to Mark's killer, drew a dagger, and drove it home with five quick jabs. The guard yanked the body down and cast it aside for somebody to collect. Then he went over to Mark's cell, opened it, and dragged Mark to the cross.

Michael thrashed and struggled, kicking and yanking, trying to break free from the guards, but after so long without food or water he was much to weak to escape their grasp.

"You want to watch so badly?" one of the guards said. "Very well, let's see how it goes." They stopped and one grabbed Michael's cheeks and pointed him directly at the cross where Mark was being shackled.

"No," Michael said. "Please." He didn't want to watch. He didn't think he could bear to see this again.

The guards laughed and held him firm.

A young woman emerged from the gate. Michael didn't recognize her. Did she know Mark? The judge threw a battle axe into the arena. She heaved the axe to her side and, without hesitation, hacked off Mark's legs.

Mark shrieked in agony but the crowd's cheers drowned out the noise.

Sarah hacked off his arms next. His torso pulled away, separating from the socket and tumbling to the ground. Then the woman chopped off his head.

Michael finally managed to break free and sprinted across the arena. He grabbed the sword he had tossed aside and brandished it at the guards approaching Mark's mangled corpse.

"Don't touch him!" he shouted.

His rebellion was short-lived. Within moments, something hit him hard in the back of the head and everything went black.

Chapter 1

When Michael came to, he was just outside the city gates. The sun was rising, but instead of the icy blue-white light from the day before, the orb bled an eerie electric pink into the sky. Not far off, Michael heard the crowds in the colosseum still roaring for blood.

He turned over and sat up. He was certain his nose was broken, but he didn't care. Twice now he had seen Mark die, murdered before his very own eyes, and he wasn't able to stop it either time. He began to weep but his desiccated tear ducts produced no tears. After a moment, he pulled himself together and looked back at the city of Gehenna. Had they really just let him go after all that? Was the colosseum just some sort of test of his character? If it was, he had nearly failed and doomed himself. Once again, Mark had saved his life. He shook his head in wonder. Even from beyond the grave....How could he have ever taken his friend for granted?

Michael stood, aching all over, and began stumbling away from the city. He didn't want to take a chance and risk the judge changing his mind and sending riders out to recapture him. He just wanted to leave the awful city behind and forget it ever existed, though he very much doubted that would be possible. Didn't he carry the filth of that city inside him? Didn't everybody to one extent or another?

Ahead of him, rust-red dunes, rocks and thinning fields of brambles led out into nowhere. He was still in the same barren and lost place he had entered the day before—but anything was better than Gehenna. If he was going to die, he'd rather die a clean death out here in the desert, the sun burning away the rottenness of the city that still clung to him.

He trudged along resolutely. A flock of vultures circled overhead, waiting for him to fall over and die. He still hadn't eaten and no water had touched his lips for two full days. He kept walking, though it was becoming increasingly difficult. His lips were so dry that they bled. His tongue had taken on a disturbing glue-like texture. The desert heat burned his nostrils when he breathed and his throat cried out for moisture.

He kept walking.

He could smell himself—not just body odor but dried feces, vomit, and urine as well. He tasted old blood mixed with echoes of the decay from the cells. He ran his tongue along his teeth again and again, hoping to get rid of the taste, but it lingered nonetheless.

He kept walking.

His joints began to ache. He tripped over nothing, falling head-long into the grit. He tripped over his own feet, his body numb. He reached up to wipe sweat off his face and was surprised to find blood mingling with the sweat on the back of his hand. Whether the wound had come from a guard's fist or one of his falls he wasn't sure, but at this point what did it matter? All he felt was a constant pain: no increase, no decrease.

Finally, he couldn't walk any farther. His body simply gave up and he fell to the ground, choking and coughing. His abdominal muscles spasmed and cramped and he retched, though nothing came out. He coughed and sputtered, his entire body shaking. This was it. He couldn't go keep going. He probably couldn't even stand back up if he tried. And what would be the point in trying, anyway? There was nothing on the horizon in any direction. No shade, no water, no civilization. There was, quite literally, no hope of escaping this desert. He sat, exhausted. He felt like he was in a trance—conscious yet hypnotized, fighting the urge to lean just so slightly to one side, just take a moment to lay on the—

Just take a moment to rest his eyes—

Just—

No. Well, just take a brief nap. Just a minute. Just take a moment to lay over and—

But just as this exhaustion was taking over, a familiar voice whispered in Michael's ear.

"You have to keep moving."

He could have sworn it was Mark, but he looked around and saw no one. Not a soul. Still, the voice gave him the strength he needed to stand once more.

And to keep walking.

If he died here, what would happen to his body? The thought kept running through his mind again and again as he considered the possibility that anyone, anywhere, would ever find his remains out in this place. Would his parents ever know? Would his bleached bones be utterly unidentifiable? Maybe it was better that way. Maybe it was better to simply disappear.

He kept walking.

He would dry up like a mummy. Particle by particle, his skin would slough away, then his muscle tissue, and eventually his bones, wearing down to dust, becoming part of the desert sands. Not a trace would be left of Michael Seymour and no one would remember his name. Except, perhaps, the figure just now approaching.

Michael stopped in his tracks. Surely he was hallucinating. A moment ago there had been no one, but now, appearing out of the shimmering bands of heat, a man was approaching. On foot this time, no horse and no sword. When the man got close enough for Michael to see him clearly, he knew for sure he was hallucinating.

Because the man was Mark.

Michael blinked. Mark was dead. Twice dead, both times right in front of him.

"You're a mirage," Michael said. "You're not real."

"Who are you calling a mirage? I'm as real as you are, Michael."

Michael still didn't quite know how to process this. "...Mark?"

Mark rolled his eyes and said, "Yeah, it's me, you bozo. Now come on and follow me. You don't want to die here."

"But you're dead."

"So you can trust me when I say you don't want to be. Get moving. Help is on the way."

Michael struggled to his feet, unable to do anything but follow. He had told himself he would listen to Mark from now on and he wasn't about to go back on his word.

He kept walking.

Chapter 8

After uncountable hours of barely keeping one foot in front of the other, and only managing that based on Mark's constant encouragement, Michael saw another mirage. Across the dunes, five men rode camels at a leisurely pace. They were approaching, but not with any great urgency, so Michael tried to suppress the instinctive fear that gripped him at the sight of more mounted figures. These men and women did not wear armor like the riders from Gehenna. Instead, they wore white robes which draped loosely off their arms and headscarves which shielded their faces from the desert sun. The camels plodded along, their riders' robes flapping in the dry wind. Despite their seemingly innocent appearance, Michael still considered running. But then the world in front of him shifted. A wave of heat shimmered across the horizon and when it dissipated it left behind sparkling pools of clear water by the riders. In the distance Michael heard the gurgling and lapping of water in a brook.

Michael looked to Mark to confirm that what he was seeing was, in fact, real, but Mark only spread his hands as if to say *I don't know, man.*

Still, mirage or real, the sight of water filled Michael with a burst of new energy. He ran toward the pools and the camels gathered around them, willing his legs to keep moving beneath him though they were practically numb with exhaustion by now. But as he approached, the water vanished and only the camels and the robed figures remained, riding away from him just fast enough to gradually outpace Michael. He felt as though the sand was sucking him in, clutching at his feet. He ran slower and slower.

"Wait," he croaked. Then again, louder: "Wait!"

One of the riders in the rear of the caravan looked back and her camel stopped, even as the other riders continued forward towards their unknown destination. Michael ran as fast as he could, sure that the camel would vanish the moment he got close. But when he caught up to it, it remained. Spent, Michael collapsed at the camel's feet. He looked up at the rider standing over him, a Middle Eastern woman whose face was dark and burned from the cruel sun.

"Why are you walking across the desert?" she said. "And why didn't you bring any water?"

"Water?" Michael begged, hearing only the last word. He cupped his dirty hands in supplication.

The nomad nodded, dug into her pack, and pulled out a leather pouch which she tossed to Michael. He fumbled to remove the cork and drank the water in big gulps, barely saving time for breathing in between the desperate swallows.

"Don't drink too fast. It will make you sick."

Michael restrained himself to smaller gulps with no small degree of difficulty. When he had drained every last drop in the pouch, he thanked the rider and asked where he was.

"I'm not sure I understand," she said. "You don't know where you are?"

"Well, you're speaking English, so I guess that narrows it down," he said.

She cocked her head. "Pardon? I don't speak this...English? Certainly you mean, 'You're speaking Aravi'?"

Michael just stared, not sure how to process this information. Weren't they speaking English? Or was his brain simply processing it that way? But if they were really speaking a language he'd never head of before, how on earth could he understand it—never mind speak it himself! Then again, so many strange things had happened already, what was the harm in a few more? Perhaps it was better to just go with the flow and agree with this nice woman who had offered him the first drink of water he had tasted in days.

"The sun has certainly gotten to your head," the woman said. She reached out for the now empty pouch and he handed it back.

"Thank you. I thought I was going to die," Michael said.

"It is a good thing we were passing through here or you would have."

It occurred to Michael that the rider had neither glanced at nor acknowledged the presence of Mark, who stood only a few feet away. He wasn't certain whether she couldn't see him or simply didn't consider him worth her attention.

"I'm just trying to get out of the desert," he said.

"Where did you come from?"

Michael hesitated, sensing that his answer would not be received especially well. The sorts of people he had seen in the fortress were... not the types one ordinarily wanted to associate with. But he knew of no other place to name, and besides this woman would without a doubt know if he lied to her.

"Gehenna," he said.

"Gehenna?" she repeated, astonished. "That place is forbidden. I have never known anyone who managed to leave that foul place once they entered its walls. You must be an uncommon man indeed."

Michael straightened his back, trying to look uncommon, to feel special deep in his heart. But he felt Mark's eyes on him and he knew, without looking, what expression he would find on Mark's face. The same one he had worn during their last argument. It seemed like years ago that he had boasted just how unique he was and the words rang so childish in his memory now. He looked up at the rider.

"Not uncommon," he said. "Just lucky. And right now I just want to go home."

"Where is your home?"

"Las Cruces, New Mexico," Michael said. Then, when the woman offered only a blank look, he added, "The United States of America?"

"I've never heard of that place," she said, sympathy clear in her voice.

Her camel emitted a snuffle that sounded all too much like mocking laughter. But camels couldn't laugh, right? Maybe the sun really *had* addled his brains. He sighed and looked over to where vultures pecked the dry carcass of...well, something. His anxiety must have shown clearly on his face.

The woman chuckled and said, "Do not worry. You will not be their meal today, my friend. Come with me. I am on a pilgrimage to a very sacred place. Perhaps you may find what you seek there."

"Thank you," Michael said. "What's your name, anyway? I want to know who to thank for saving my life."

The woman offered a small smile and a slight bow of her head, one hand to her heart, and said, "I am Yamani. And you are...?"

"Michael. Michael Seymour. Where are we going?"

"We are going to the Holy Mountain that holds the Altar of the Cup of All Good Things. I have traveled a long way and we are now only half a day's ride away." Yamani looked towards the horizon and saw that the other riders were already out of sight. "I'm on a pilgrimage to pray for the Cup of All Good Things to be righted once more."

The camel dropped its head low to the sand as though Yamani's very words had prompted it to pray in its own way.

"Sounds good to me," Michael said. A holy woman on a holy quest. That beat Gehenna a thousand times over. A million times. "Let's go!"

Yamani looked him up and down and grimaced.

"Yes, but first..." She dug into her pack and took out a clean cloth and a corked ceramic bottle of ointment. "Take this and use it and the sand to clean yourself. And please, leave your soiled clothes here—I have spare garments for you."

When Michael hesitated, she laughed.

"Don't worry, I'll turn my eyes toward the Altar. You will have as much privacy as you need." With that, she wheeled her camel around and faced dutifully away. Michael looked around for Mark but he had vanished from sight. Whether out of politeness or some other force, Michael couldn't say. He stepped out of his filthy clothes and got to work, scrubbing every inch of his body until his skin ached. The ointment stung his wounds but, moments later, sent a cool, soothing sensation through them.

When he was through, he felt like a new man. The stench of Gehenna had left him almost entirely, and what little of it remained was easily overpowered by the rich, herbal smell of the ointment. He saw a long white robe neatly folded atop a pair of sandals behind Yamani's camel and put them on. Simply wearing clean clothes again was an indescribable pleasure, nearly as satisfying as the drink of water he had taken moments ago. For the first time in days, he felt like a human being. He felt like Michael Seymour.

He kicked sand over his old, ruined clothes and shoes and hoped the desert would reclaim them quickly. The he stepped alongside Yamani's camel and she nodded at him.

"I don't know how I can ever repay you for your kindness," Michael said.

Yamani extended a hand. "Living is its own reward. Come with me, Michael. We will journey to the Holy Mountain and, if you wish it, you can continue your journey from there."

Michael climbed awkwardly onto the camel's back, behind Yamani. The perch was much higher off the ground than he had expected, and he found himself suddenly nervous about falling and breaking something.

"You've never ridden a camel before, I see," Yamani said.

"I've never even seen one in real life before."

The camel grunted and started to move. Its long lumbering stride made Michael lurch and sway. After finally gaining his balance, he said, "I still don't know how to thank you."

"There is no need to thank me, my friend. I welcome anyone who comes to wish for a better world."

A better world. What would that mean? Surely it meant something better than this vast, lethal desert and the inexplicable horrors it contained. But Michael realized this might be Yamani's home and stopped himself from saying this out loud.

They rode for hours, and eventually the sun began to settle between a pair of dunes on the horizon. Despite the constant shaking and bumping with each stride the camel took, Michael found himself growing drowsy, and finally dozed off. He startled awake, somewhat embarrassed that he had been sleeping slumped against Yamani's back. The bright red dunes had been replaced by a fine black sandy plain, spreading out from horizon to horizon as if the landscape Michael had trekked through for so long had never existed at all.

Yamani chuckled and said, "You're awake, my friend! Do not worry. We will arrive at our destination soon."

"Is that it?" Michael said after his eyes adjusted to the dusk. He pointed to an island of lights amid the black plain—something that looked like civilization. As they drew closer, he saw that what he was looking at was a drive-in movie theater. Countless nomads, some with camels and some without, lounged next to speakers arranged around a screen. Various wealthy sheiks relaxed in air-conditioned golden Cadillacs. Among the Cadillacs was one yellow Hummer.

"They are offspring of Gehenna," Yamani said under her breath. "Unbefitting of the blessing from the Cup of All Good Things."

Michael squinted at the screen as they passed by and was surprised to see somebody who looked just like himself, but a few years older. The man was in the prime of his athletic career, performing in what seemed to be a very intense gymnastic competition. The crowd stared silently, in awe of the Adonis performing in front of them. The athlete on the screen sprinted across the gym floor at astonishing speed, then leaped, bounced, and whirled his body in in a crisp, double twisting dismount and landing precisely on a pad. The crowd burst into cheers and the man, who appeared able to see and hear them despite being a projection, raised his arms and bowed again and again.

"Wow," Michael whispered.

"A wicked place, to be certain," Yamani said. "Many beautiful things in this world are not what they seem. Not every nexus of evil is as blatant as Gehenna."

The plain began to incline and the cinema and its patrons faded into nothing. In the distance ahead, a range of high mountains touched the sky, a dark violet band against the navy dusk. They weren't Michael's mountains, but they reminded him of home nonetheless. Their familiarity—and their unfamiliarity—sent a needle through his heart. Somehow, some way, he would find his way back. He had to.

The two riders crested a small hill and Michael was astonished by the sight below. In the valley, long lines of men and women walked across the desert in the glow of torches, all of them heading in the same direction, toward a mountain which rose from the center of the valley.

"They come from every part of this great land to visit the Altar of the Cup," Yamani said. "In the time of my forefathers, there was great prosperity. The Cup of All Good Things was the center of our lives. Our fields were lush and fertile and gave us all we needed. Then a great wind came and the Cup of All Good Things fell. Its contents spilled out and the land became blighted. Droughts, floods, and sandstorms tormented our lives and those of our descendants. We became a people without hope, and we left our lands to wander the earth, seeking the blessings that may have been spilt out upon another land. But we have found none, so many of us return here. All of these people wish for the Cup of All Good Things to be righted, so things will return to the way they once were."

Michael thought about Wendy, Mark, his running career, his health—all the things he wished he could go back and put right again. Things which could not be put right.

"I wish for the same thing," he said. "But I'm not sure it's possible. Some changes are permanent."

Yamani looked shocked, then her face fell, as though she felt sorry for Michael. "You do not understand," she said.

"I guess I don't. But...I want to." What he meant to say was *I want more than anything for you to be right. I want to believe I can undo everything that has happened.*

She sighed. "The falling of the Cup of All Good Things is a curse, Michael. We did not face hardship while the Cup stood upright. We wanted for nothing. We knew neither hunger nor drought nor plague. I am certain that, when the Cup is righted again, all these things will evaporate—poof—like water in the desert. This is how it was before and how it will be again."

Michael opened his mouth to point out the flaws in Yamani's

thinking, but he thought better of it. He used to believe that curses could only hurt people if they believed in them and their power. That was back when he believed he would always win, always beat whatever came his way, with no help at all. Now he wasn't so sure. And he'd seen some strange things in this world, wherever it might be. Maybe curses had real power after all. He decided to keep his mouth shut and just observe. If Yamani was right, and the Cup would right all wrongs, maybe he should try to right it, too. Maybe, miraculously, his life would go back to normal.

But did he want what had passed for "normal"?

Of course he wanted Mark to be alive again. Of course he hoped that maybe, somehow, he'd be able to talk to Wendy and convince her to give him a second chance. Of course he'd like to be rid of his illness. But if going back to all of that meant never growing as a person, never understanding why Mark couldn't stand him sometimes and never treating Wendy with the respect she deserved—was it worth it? He wasn't sure anymore. He needed a new normal. A better normal.

"Show me the Cup," Michael said.

They descended the zigzagging trail etched into the side of the slanted rock face and soon came to a plateau about halfway up the mountain. Masses of people were gathered here and a long procession climbed up the thin path to the stone altar at the top.

"The Holy Mountain," Yamani said.

All across the plateau, pilgrims chanted in unison. Their voices rose to a crescendo and fell like a receding wave and then swelled again as they repeated the same chant over and over again. Michael felt like he was close to a huge waterfall, the noise of the chanting reverberating through his body. He wondered again if he could be wrong about the Cup. Maybe it really was something magical, something blessed, to create such a huge and moving response from so many people.

When they were half a mile away from the altar, Yamani pulled back on the reins and her camel stopped just as suddenly, expressing displeasure with tiny snorts of air. She ordered it to its knees with a barked command, then dismounted and helped Michael off its back. Michael turned around and around, watching the throngs of people in amazement. They were standing, sitting, kneeling, some had their eyes closed, while others kept their gazes fixed on the mountain peak. Almost everyone was chanting. Those who weren't were busy tending to their camps, small clusters of tends and lean-tos set up around pitiful fires. Yamani guided Michael through the crowd. At the foot of the Holy Mountain itself, Yamani lay out a carpet, set up a goat-hide lean-to, and started a small fire with some dried camel dung. A young man came running toward them, carrying a heavy bag of supplies and various provisions.

"Michael, my friend," Yamani said, "this is my servant, Yusef."

Yamani took the bag from Yusef and the two of them began making camp. She did not ask Michael to help, so he wandered around awkwardly, just watching the people around him. The continuous chant from the pilgrims had faded into a constant, monotonous drone in the background and he wondered if they would keep at it all night (and if they did, how he would manage to sleep). Still, there was something undeniably admirable about the dedication on display here. Whether or not the stories about the Cup were true, these people really believed in something with all their hearts. Could Michael say the same?

When the camp was ready, Yamani invited Michael to sit beside her on the carpet by the fire. She broke a loaf of dark rich bread in two and offered him a chunk. He had been so focused on his thirst that he hadn't realized, until now, just how profoundly hungry he was. He hadn't eaten for what felt like weeks. He tore into the yeasty bread and watched Yusef brew tea over the fire. Then he stopped eating in mid-bite, realizing that Yamani, his host, hadn't yet eaten but was watching him with a careful eye. Michael swallowed twice before saying, "Thank you, Yamani."

"Thank the One who feeds us all," Yamani said, bowing and touching his forehead.

"Yeah, sure," Michael said flippantly. If he was honest with himself, he wasn't sure what he thought about a higher power, especially after all he had been through. What part of it was God responsible for? If he was going to thank God for the good things—like water, bread, and the kindness of strangers—should he also blame God for the bad things as well—like Gehenna or his illness or Mark's death?

Yamani, evidently, didn't share these concerns. She was staring at him rather coldly and he chuckled nervously, suddenly worried that his casual remark had offended her.

"I mean, of course, thanks to the One," he said quickly, but it was too late. Yamani could see right through him. She held his stare for a moment, then turned towards Yusef who had just set two cups of tea on a serving tray.

"Do not worry about the tea, Yusef. We won't be needing it."

Michael's heart sank.

Yusef pivoted and walked right back out of the tent. Yamani closed a bag that obviously held more food and pushed it toward the rest of her bags in the corner of the tent. Michael cursed himself for having cheated his growling stomach out of a full meal. He glanced outside the tent in time to see Yusef throw back one of the teas in a single gulp and toss the contents of the other cup to the side.

Yamani and Michael finished their bread slowly, silently, chewing and savoring every bite of the heavy multi-grain bread, washing it down with great draughts of sweet water from Yamani's leather flask. Michael wanted to say something to get back into his host's good graces, but worried that whatever he said might end up digging him into an even deeper hole than the one in which he now found himself.

When they finished, Yamani gazed at the Holy Mountain, and Michael couldn't help but notice the way her eyes glimmered when looking at it, as if she were enraptured by nothing more than being in its presence. It seemed as though she were waiting for the Mountain to speak. Perhaps literally.

"I have traveled for six weeks," she said, not so much to Michael as to the Mountain. "I am ready."

Then she turned to Michael and took ahold of his arm. "Follow me to the Altar. Come and wish with me."

Michael did as he was asked and followed her out of the tent. The people looked different now that night had set in in earnest. They were people who had come from everywhere, from different lands, from every region and valley, to wish for the curse to be lifted and for the Cup to be righted once again. In the glare and the dust of the day, they had been pilgrims. In the mystical glow of a thousand smoking torches, they became supplicants, dedicated worshippers.

Michael and Yamani walked as quickly as they could up the lava stone steps that led to the summit. As Michael got closer to the top, the breathtaking view only got better. In the valley below strings of torches carried by incoming pilgrims glowed like strands of golden beads thrown across a black velvet desert. Their chanting grew louder as they approached the Mountain. They knelt at its base, eyes lifted, wishing aloud at the top of their lungs for the Cup to be righted once more. Tears flowed down their cheeks and glittered in the torchlight. They pled to become one with the Holy Mountain so its spirit would move the earth to right the Cup and end the curse. Some had brought offerings in the form of flowers, fruit, the carcasses of animals of all sizes, symbols engraved in gold and stone and wood, and a nose-wrenching variety of smoldering incense. Some read aloud from ancient scrolls, and others leaped and howled madly, wishing, pleading, entreating, begging and promising to change their ways forever if only the Cup would be righted.

Finally, Michael reached the peak and saw the Cup for the first time. To his surprise, this relic, this object of worship from that immense crowd below, looked exactly like a big teacup from an amusement park ride, though it appeared to be made of solid gold. It lay on its side, resting against its ornately curved handle.

Michael looked around at the supplicants who had prostrated themselves at the summit and was at first moved by their passion. But the more sincere they were in their wishes for the Cup to be righted, the more he was irritated by the way they ignored the obvious. Beside him, Yamani dropped to her knees and began to wish with such intensity that Michael could feel her words like heat radiating from her very soul.

"For the people," she wished, tears springing to her eyes. "For the land and the forests, oh, how I wish the Cup were righted!"

The hair stood up on the back of Michael's neck and his breath caught in his throat, but still he couldn't get past the fact that the Cup was right there in front of all of them and nobody seemed willing to approach it. He shrugged and walked up to the big golden Cup, not entirely sure what he was going to do until he did it. A shadow which he quickly realized was Mark appeared among the worshippers and Michael froze. He had thought the hallucination would have left for good after he drank water, but apparently not. Mark was shaking his head wildly and speaking, but his words were drowned out by the rhythmic chants of the people. Well, if he was trying to say something important, he could come up here and say it.

Without a word, Michael grasped the rim of the Cup and squatted down to brace himself. The noise of the crowd suddenly dropped to nothing. In a stunned silence, all they did was watch.

Michael drew a deep breath, then pulled upward on the rim with all his strength. Slowly, carefully, he raised the rim until he could push the Cup over. It landed with an echoing thud, once again sitting perfectly upright.

Chapter 9

For the longest time, the only thing Michael could hear was the wind rushing down the Mountain. The crowd stood, dumbfounded, and for a moment Michael wondered if they would be angry with him. Then one man fell to his knees and cried out, "The Great Prophet has come!"

One after another the people dropped to their knees and prostrated themselves before him.

"The Messiah! The Great Prophet!" they cried.

Michael didn't know what to think, much less what to actually say or do. He wanted to tell these people that he only did what any one of them could have done, but the words were frozen on his lips. He watched, helpless as the people began to worship him.

"He was a stranger lost in the desert," Yamani cried out. "I gave him water and shared my bread with him, and now he has fulfilled all of our wishes. This is Michael the Prophet!"

The crowd chanted, "Prophet Mikail!"

An instant later, they surrounded him, grabbing at his robe, touching his face, chanting his name. In a perverse way, it was just what he'd always dreamed of. But it was wrong. He hadn't earned any of this. He wasn't special.

"Hey, wait a minute," Michael said. "Wait a minute!"

Ignoring his protests, the crowd lifted him up and carried him aloft, passing him from hand to hand, a boat carried on the sea of the masses to the bottom of the Mountain. They lay him down on bright pillows and brought rich carpets and clothing and all kinds of fine food. They built bonfires so large the heat radiated out for a hundred yards. The camps burst into a flurry of activity as the people wrote new liturgies and rituals centered around "Prophet Mikail."

Michael rested his chin on the palm of his hand as people came in and out of the tent, bowing low to greet him. Most skirted around him, nervous, as though they weren't sure how close they were allowed to get. Others were bold and just stared, full of daring and wonder. He felt like he was in a zoo. He wanted to tell these people there had been a terrible misunderstanding but he worried the moment for that had already passed, and with every new supplicant he became more and more certain of this fact.

Well, at least he would have some good food to eat eventually, if the people ever stopped running around to get things set up for him. Who could have predicted that he would go from wandering through the desert, starving and filthy, to lounging on a soft pile of pillows while other people scrambled to care for his needs? He wished he could attribute his reversal of fortune to something he had done, some feat of strength or speed or bravery—but in truth he had only been lucky.

Every once in a while, Michael heard a strangled bleat or bawl emerge from the night and he knew that a goat or lamb was being slaughtered in his name. This, in particular, made him uncomfortable, but once more he feared he would offend the pilgrims gravely by asking them to stop. Although Michael had never been a real animal lover, he didn't like to picture the way these travelers got real close and personal with their food. One second they were gently patting its head and the next they had slit its throat. It was a merciful death, given how unexpected and sudden it all was—and definitely more humane than the filthy factory farms in America—but Michael wondered nervously if the pilgrims were just as unpredictable with their prophets as they were with their animals. He sure didn't want his throat to be slit after a nice meal, just when he'd grown used to the nice little pats on his head.

Finally, people began bringing food. A few men brought long tables and set them up in endless rows. The piles of food grew and grew. Michael soon grew ravenous, smelling the delicious aroma of spicy meat cooking on spits over open fires. Then, at last, the feasting began. Michael had never before tasted food as good as this—though his hunger probably played an outsized role in this. Plates laden with spiced ground lamb, sausages, rice wrapped in grape leaves, hummus, eggplant, yogurt, and more sauces than Michael could count were passed around and around and each dish Michael sampled tasted better than the last. Everywhere, men and women ate and drank and danced in joyous celebration. He wasn't sure how he could know such a thing, but he sensed that they were singing songs they hadn't sung for a long, long time.

They served him and fussed over him, feeding him and entertaining him. Although he knew he wasn't the savior or messiah they were looking for, he couldn't deny that he was enjoying the feast. Yamani sat on a pillow beside him, enshrined as Michael's first disciple, and the people knelt before her as well.

"Michael," Yamani said. "They want you to speak to them. They desire to hear your words of wisdom, of prophesy, of leadership."

"I don't know what to say, Yamani," Michael whispered. "I don't know the first thing about leading people. I'm not a prophet. I'm not—"

Yamani shook her head, and for the first time it occurred to Michael that she knew full well he was no messiah. "The people need a leader," she whispered back. "You righted the Cup. You restored their hope. Prophet or not, you have made yourself a symbol of that new hope. And now you want to waste all that and disappoint those who have traveled for miles to be here?"

Michael squeezed his eyes shut and pressed his palms to his forehead. What could he do to make Yamani understand where he was coming from?

"Yamani, I'm not a good man. I'm bad news for everyone around me. Everyone who depends on me finds out sooner or later that they've made a terrible, terrible mistake. But I don't pay for that mistake—they do. So I just don't think it's a very good idea to let *all* these people start relying on me."

"We wished for the Cup to be righted," Yamani said. "We prayed for it to happen, day after day and night after night. And what happened? You righted it. So whether you like it or not, these people already depend on you. You are just frightened and unprepared but the truth is all around us. You are their hope-bearer. You owe them whatever hope you can give."

"I can't give them hope without reason." The words he couldn't say were on the tip of his tongue: *I can't even give myself hope, how could I possibly give it to anyone else?* "All I did was lift the Cup."

Yamani glared at Michael. "That is what you say. But when these people look at you, do you know what they see? They don't see a ragged, sunburned, feces-stained vagrant staggering through the desert, as I saw. They see a man who has fulfilled their deepest wishes and set the world right again. Given the strength of their belief, I do not believe it matters what you think." Yamani looked him up and down and frowned. "Besides, who is to say you are not blessed? To escape Gehenna, to wander helplessly through the desert and find water exactly when you most needed it, to arrive at the Holy Mountain just when these people most needed you.... These are not ordinary coincidences. Though you are certainly no prophet, you have nonetheless clearly been blessed by the Lord, though for reasons I cannot fathom."

"I'm not blessed," Michael said, feeling weary. Everything Yamani said made sense, but he couldn't imagine actually taking on the burden of guiding all these people through whatever challenges were to come. He had only been in their world for...a day? Two? Three? Time here moved in the strangest ways. A single instant might seem to go on interminably, while an entire day could pass in the blink of an eye.

"I'm not more blessed than you are, Yamani. Or that camel over there, the one that Yusef is leading to the water. The people need to find their hope within themselves. They can't rely on others who are bound to disappoint. They can't rely on a big golden cup."

"You are wrong," Yamani said, firmly. "Look at the people, Michael. They are not afraid of life anymore. They are free from their curses. They have been saved! And now they need direction. They need a leader."

Michael stood. "I can hardly keep myself together. I'm not the leader they need."

"Then what do you plan to do?" Yamani demanded. People began to take notice and she dropped her voice. "Will you abandon them? Destroy the hopes of thousands of people?"

Michael didn't have an answer.

"I can't bear to see my people fall again," Yamani said. "I won't. Please. Please give your position, your *responsibility*, some thought."

Michael nodded and retreated into the tent. He had hoped Yamani would understand. If not Yamani, who else did he have to talk to? Nobody. As if on cue, Mark appeared again, casually leaning on the pile of pillows, trying to eat some grapes that just faded through his mouth.

Michael fought off a smile. He was grateful to see his friend again, whether the phantom in front of him was real or not. Mark paused in his attempts to eat the grapes.

"I tried to warn you, man," he said. "These things always have more catches than they first appear. And don't even try to lie to yourself and say you can actually be the savior to these people. Even you can't be *that* full of yourself."

Michael winced. "You're right. You've always been right. I should have listened to you." He took a deep breath. There was more he needed to say, things he had wished he could say since the stabbing. "I've been an asshole and I'm surprised you stayed around as long as you did. You deserved better. I'm sorry."

Mark kept his face neutral, but something flickered beneath the surface—something like disappointment. "You ass. You know you can't just apologize for something and make it better. I died for you, man. And what have you done with that? Tricked all these people into worshipping you because you thought you knew better than them? You act like you've changed, but that's exactly something the Michael Seymour I knew would have done. Congratulations, you're the messiah—are you happy now?"

Michael tried to speak but his words caught in his throat and he realized he had nothing to say. As usual, Mark was completely correct.

Mark sighed and his expression changed to one of sympathy rather than judgment. "Michael, man. What are you doing here?"

"I don't know."

"Well, you'd best start figuring that out."

Eventually, the people's songs died down as the night wore on and the people realized that Michael would not emerge from the tent to speak to them. He knew he couldn't just hide out in there forever, but the thought of stepping back outside paralyzed him. Eventually, propped on his luxurious pillows and unwilling to move, he drifted into an anxious, fitful sleep.

He woke the next morning, alone. Mark was nowhere to be seen. Michael sat up, stretched, and realized he actually felt pretty good. All that worrying... maybe it was for nothing. Maybe he could simply trade for a camel or something and ride away in peace. He stood, put on a freshly washed robe that was folded neatly on the floor beside him and stepped out of the tent, whereupon his hopes were instantly shattered.

Immediately he was assaulted by the noise of the people.

"Hail the Prophet! Hail the Messiah!"

Somehow, the crowd was even larger than it had been the night before. They surrounded the tent, their arms outstretched toward him. A woman held her baby out toward him, beseeching him. "My baby! My baby! Please bless my baby!"

For a moment, Michael was horrified. But then he looked out over the sea of expectant faces. If he *didn't* do this, would they think he was dooming this child? But what would they think when they no longer believed he was their prophet, as they inevitably would? Well, he would worry about that later. At the moment, the mob must be satisfied. He pressed his hand against the baby's forehead and declared, "Be blessed!"

The women shrieked in delight and held her baby toward the sky. "My baby has been blessed by the Prophet!" She wandered through the masses, holding the baby aloft for everyone to see. "My child shall be a holy child!"

"Good Prophet?"

Michael turned to see an old man leaning toward him, holding onto one edge of a coat. Another man slightly behind him also held onto the coat.

"He took my coat!" the old man said.

"I was cold!" the other man said. Both looked to Michael for some sort of resolution.

"Do you have another coat?" Michael asked the older man, noticing he was wearing one very much like the one he was holding.

"The one I'm wearing," the old man said.

"And do you have a coat of your own?" Michael asked the second man.

"No."

"Then give him the coat," Michael said to the old man. "Don't let your neighbor go cold."

"Very well," the old man said, and he released the garment. "I accept your wisdom, O Great Prophet." He bowed at the waist and backed away, his expression a little sullen but not angry. The other man was already pulling on the coat, bowing as he thanked Michael and slipping into the crowd, leaving space for more people to press close in his absence.

Was leading as simple as that? For all his worrying, that had actually been pretty easy. But if they really would do whatever he said, the responsibility on his shoulders was even more enormous than he had suspected. What was a prophet or messiah supposed to teach? What kind of values was he supposed to propagate? And did Michael Seymour possess any of the qualities worth instilling in others? His mother would have said that kindness, generosity, and compassion were of the utmost importance. But despite her insistence that those were the qualities to value, Michael had to admit he'd never thought much about whether he had them or not. Mark had suggested he didn't, and Michael was inclined to believe him.

Before another pilgrim could approach him and pose their own dilemma, Yamani emerged from the masses. She grabbed Michael by the arm and led him through the crowd.

"Make way! Make way! Make way for the Prophet." Her shouts carved a narrow path through the bodies like a river running through a canyon. She led Michael to her tent, where Yusef had prepared mint tea and food—olives, hummus and pita bread. She motioned toward the spread, saying, "We should talk."

Michael sat and took the cup of tea that Yusef poured him. But before he could even take a sip, an elderly man dressed in the finest gold-trimmed attire stepped into the tent.

"Good morning, Prophet Michael. Oh, and good morning, Yamani," he added.

"Good morning, Fahid," Yamani replied. "Can you not see that we are busy here?"

Fahid bowed his head and said, "The tribal elders desire your presence and your counsel, Michael."

"And what are we going to discuss this time?" Yamani said.

"That is to be determined at the meeting," Fahid said. "We hope to see you both there." He bowed and exited the tent.

Yamani turned to Michael with a deep sigh. "Fahid leads another tribe. He can be... tiring."

Michael raised an eyebrow. "I didn't know you led a tribe."

"I do."

"So I have ask you a question, with all due respect. Why do you dress like the common people? Why don't you dress like Fahid?"

"Because it is hard to understand the position of others if you set yourself apart from them. People tend to trust people who look and act like they do, who dress like they do. You can serve people better if they trust you." She grabbed a ceremonial sash from a bag, set her glass of tea back on the serving tray, and stood up to wrap the sash around her waist. "But we must go to the council meeting. Come, Michael."

The tribal meeting was a circus. It began with a lengthy series of hypothetical disputes among the leaders over Michael's legitimacy as the long-awaited prophet. They also discussed the thought that if he was the prophet, what the implications would be concerning their leaderships of the various tribes, as well as the ins and outs of every law in their many books. Generally every resolution only further secured their power, which in turn only furthered the amount of tributes required of the people.

Yamani's contributions to the discussions were brilliant, but mostly went unnoticed or dismissed by her male peers. She stood out as the single kind leader in the council, taking into account the people's needs instead of just the Council's.

Pilgrims also consulted the council over legal disputes, but, now that the Prophet was among the Council, the line of people seeking advice stretched a mile long and few of their complaints were actually heard. Michael was instructed not to speak, and the council spoke on his behalf. He didn't particularly mind, although it did add to the drudgery, which was already considerable.

The council meeting went on from sunup to sundown and even then showed no signs of stopping. After hours and hours of apparently pointless discussions, Michael was exhausted. There was no way he could keep this up. In a way, he felt like he was a prisoner, though his circumstances were admittedly much more comfortable than his previous lodging. The longer the meeting went, the clearer it became that he was merely being used as a tool for the tribal leaders to secure more power. He had to get away from these people.

Finally, as the dusk was deepening and Fahid was mid-ramble, Michael couldn't take it anymore. He interrupted and said, "If I may have your attention, Great Leaders of the Council."

Fahid twitched. He stared at Michael long and hard before saying with a twinge of annoyance in his voice, "And what does our *Great* Prophet have to contribute to this discussion?"

Michael tried to collect in his mind all the lingo these charlatans threw around as though they were actually talking about something. "*Wise* leaders," he said. "I have been tasked by the Provider of All Good Things to determine how to help progress the peace and prosperity of our people and return us to our lands."

"And just what have you determined?" Fahid said, impatient.

"Tomorrow shall be a day of fasting for every pilgrim under the Holy Mountain."

"A fast?" Yamani said.

Michael nodded. "Let every person be confined to their own tent during the day tomorrow. Neither food nor drink shall pass through their lips, unless they be ill, an infant, pregnant, or elderly. Let them consider what their life was like before the Cup was righted, before the rightful order was restored, and before the council returned the lives of the people to the way things were before the Cup fell."

Michael couldn't believe all the crap that was falling from his lips. The grandiosity of it all turned his stomach but he had to do what he had to do. He could almost feel Mark shaking his head at him, and only hoped his friend understood where he was going with this. But Mark hadn't appeared all day, perhaps still angry with Michael. It was hard to tell when the phantom would come and go, or why. In any case, it didn't matter what the phantom thought. Michael had to get the hell out of here. Not just this camp, but this strange world in which he found himself stranded. More and more, his thoughts were consumed with his home, his parents, and, most of all, Wendy. She was like a ghost in his head now. Had she really existed? Was she really that important a part of his life? He wanted to go home even if nobody wanted him there anymore. He could find a way to apologize, right? Not manipulating his way out of what he had done, but actually making things right again. Somehow.

"And what would be the *purpose* of such an observance?" Fahid said. "What exactly has changed in a day that the people need to reflect on?"

Michael's mind raced. "The collective memory of the people is weak and fragile. Things are easily forgotten. They do not even remember the lives they had before the Cup was righted. They must consider the peace and prosperity that the Council has brought them, now that the Great Prophet has come. Only the Council has the authority to lead the people, and only he who has righted the Cup has the authority to lead the Council."

"The Prophet has spoken!" the council-members shouted, smiling and nodding at each other, delighted.

With that, Michael rose and went back to his tent. Not long after,

Yamani ducked inside.

"I have been thinking about what to say," she said.

"Let's hear it," Michael said.

"I do not understand you, Michael. I do not understand how someone can be given such a gift and turn their nose up at it. The One Who Provides All Good Things has placed you at exactly the right place at exactly the right time but you refuse to acknowledge this. Do you feel no sense of duty to your Creator?"

Michael lowered his gaze. "Yamani," he said at last. "I am deeply sorry that I offended you earlier. I don't wish to offend you at all, my friend. But I do not believe in God."

Yamani said nothing for a long while. Michael supposed she was weighing him and finding him severely wanting. So he was surprised when she said only, "It is not required for a person to believe in the One Who Provides All Good Things for the One to work through him. Now, what are you going to do, Michael?"

Michael drew a deep breath and said, "Tomorrow, I'll fix the mistake I made. I must go back up to the Holy Mountain alone. If somebody else wishes to do what I did, they can."

Yamani said nothing but she nodded. Michael could only hope she understood. If anybody should lead these people, it should be Yamani. Righting the cup took nothing more than some thigh and bicep muscles. Yamani had plenty of both.

After Yamani went back outside, Michael paced around in his tent, thinking. What would he do after this? Where would he go? No one would want a false prophet around, must less one that tilts the Cup of All Good Things back over onto its side. He would have to leave, but had no idea what would come after that. He could only hope it would not involve more aimless, scorching wandering through the desert. That night, he slept little.

The next morning, Michael was relieved to find that the people had indeed remained in their tents as he had decreed. No crowd greeted him outside his tent, no babies were pushed in his face. The foot of the mountain was quiet and peaceful. Michael grabbed a bag of food and a skin of water from his tent and set out on his quest.

He climbed the mountain alone, with only the wind for company. When he reached the top, he looked at the sea of tents below him and wondered what this scene would look like the next day when everyone emerged and saw what he had done.

He walked to the great golden Cup and, with a resolute heave, he pushed it back onto its side. As it fell, it boomed like a bell, echoing in the valley down below. Michael froze, watching the tents for signs of life, of people emerging in consternation or anger. If they came out and saw what he had done, who knew what they would do? Crucify him? Skewer him on one of the sacrificial roasting spits?

A minute passed, then another. Nobody emerged. Nothing stirred on the plateau. Michael allowed himself a small laugh. Then he set off down the opposite side of the mountain, leaving the camp and the cup behind. He set his sights on a nearby hill where he could watch, undetected, what happened when people discovered what he had done.

"That was your big plan to fix things?"

Michael wasn't sure if he was excited or disappointed to hear that voice again. Mark.

"I can't lead them," Michael said. "You know that. You knew it the moment I was about to pick up the Cup. I just did what I could to right the situation."

Mark nodded. "I suppose your plan might work. Only one way to find out."

Michael trekked for hours and finally stopped on the hilltop, far enough to be unseen if he lay down but close enough that he could keep tabs on the camp. As he suspected, a few of the people below did not wait for sundown to emerge from their tents. From the distant hill, he watched the first few figures appear on the plateau and look in horror at the mountaintop. There were only a few shouts at first as they pointed at the fallen Cup, but more and more took up the cry as they stepped from their tents and saw that they had been betrayed. A great wail rose up from the plateau and carried to the hill on which Michael perched:

"The Cup has fallen! The Cup has fallen!"

Like a thousand ants, people swarmed up the Holy Mountain, falling on their faces before the Altar, wailing and weeping and praying for the Cup to be lifted once more.

"Where is our Prophet? Where is our Messiah?" they cried.

Michael shook his head. They were right back where they had started before he had arrived. Were they really doomed to remain in this state forever?

Then, something changed. The crowds parted to make way for a woman slowly climbing up the stairs to the Cup. It was Yamani. Without hesitation, she stepped to the Cup, braced herself, and lifted it with all her strength. It clattered as she set it upright and the sound was followed by a heavy silence. No one spoke or shouted or cheered. Then someone began to clap and another picked up the rhythm, and soon the whole crowd was applauding together.

Michael smiled. He had been right to believe in her after all. She would treat her people well with dignity and respect. Rather than restoring the proper order, she would lead them forward, and lead them to create their own blessings for themselves and each other.

Michael turned away from the Holy Mountain and looked toward the peaks in the distance, which glowed pink and gold as the sunrise struck their icy crests. They dominated and surpassed all other sights, timeless creations filled with mystery. It drew him like a siren's call to a fate he dared not even imagine.

Chapter 10

Michael made his way up the winding path towards the high peaks, the barrenness of the desert forgotten. It seemed like a magical path, nature expressing its artistry in an exquisite lushness of life. So fluid was the change that it seemed the flowers actually sprouted up out of the ground and bloomed at his feet as he walked. It seemed like the stones and trees parted before him to make his walk effortless. Green meadows flourished throughout the mountains, where birds of all colors flew in shimmering clouds over a sea of waving grass and trilled like violins in the wind. A cool breeze wafted through and the floral fragrance it carried was so fresh and delicate that Michael gasped.

"This is more like it," he said. And he began to run.

He ran and ran, recalling with each step how much joy he found in these motions when he wasn't running for his life or chasing vanishing water across an endless desert. Step after step, he accelerated and the transformation of the land accelerated around him. It morphed into such fantastic forms and colors that his mind could barely grasp it. Fantastical trees and wildflowers flitted past on either side but he didn't want to slow down long enough to get a good look at any of it, so it all blurred into a kaleidoscope of natural beauty.

When Michael at last began to slow, he couldn't say for how long he had been running, nor how far he had traveled. Somehow he suspected it wasn't so much a question of distance or time as some other, dreamlike measurement he couldn't fathom which now separated him from the Holy Mountain. By the sun's position, he had either not spent a single actual minute running or literally ran for an entire day and night without realizing it.

But what was the point in dwelling on these things anymore?

He wasn't about to find an explanation anytime soon, so he may as well just accept the peculiar rules of this new reality and worry about other things. He took a deep breath of the pleasant, flower-scented air, and continued down the path at a walk. The trees which surrounded him were mostly evergreens—sugar pines and firs and ponderosa pines and the like—but flowers bloomed along their trunks, which Michael was pretty sure wasn't normal. Huge gnarled branches, shaped and intertwined by decades, or perhaps even centuries, of growth reached their hands out to Michael in a gesture not of menace but of welcome. Butterflies of all colors and wing patterns flitted across the path and occasionally hovered just in front of Michael's face. The birdsong was unlike anything he had heard in New Mexico. So he walked, simply enjoying his journey for the first time since he arrived.

As he walked, he realized the limp he had picked up from his fall had vanished entirely. His limp was entirely gone. Wisps of mist gathered in hollow places and streams of light cut through the canopy overhead. With the sun behind him, he marveled at the huge rainbow arching above the trees, boasting colors far mor vibrant than any he had seen before. He followed the path around a grove of dark green tamarisks and found a basin among the rocks where a waterfall tumbled down to splash joyfully into a crystal pool. Grapes and fat boysenberries ripened in the sun and limbs bent under the weight of succulent fruit he couldn't even identify.

The scene was so spectacularly lovely that he couldn't suppress his joy. He whooped and ran to the edge of the pool, wondering what benevolent force could have created such a magnificent landscape. When he reached the pool, he dove in without missing a beat or even bothering to strip off his clothes. The water was chilled to perfect icy keenness by its descent from the snow-capped peaks and the shock of the cold flooded him with energy. He splashed and played like an otter for what seemed like hours.

He drank, not just gratefully, but passionately, and felt refreshed like never felt before. When he finally tired of the water, Michael climbed onto a smooth expanse of polished rock to bask in the soft sunlight. He ran his fingers through his shaggy hair and thought he could stay there forever.

Once he was dry and was done enjoying the cool breeze against his sun-warmed skin, he stood and noticed his reflection in the water. He had several days' worth of growth on his beard and his tousled hair had lengthened considerably. How long had he been here?

A sunset of crimson and gold marked the end of the day. As the evening began to cool, Michael walked around, snacking on berries from the trees and bread he had brought from the camp. Some distance from the waterfall, he found a spot sheltered from the cold night breeze by several large boulders. The stars filled the sky, an owl sang its lonely song, and a huge golden moon rose up over the valley below. Other voices of the night joined the stealth-winged hunter. Michael slipped into the dry little cleft beneath the boulders and listened in delight to the nocturnal choir.

"I like it here," he said to the trees around him, or maybe Mark, if he was listening.

As he drifted off to sleep, he thought he heard a bell. It was a sweet tone, but he was unable to tell where the sound came from, or if it was even real at all.

The dawn came only a moment later and Michael was woken by the sounds of birds celebrating the new day.

Michael rubbed his eyes to clear away the sleep then slowly stretched to loosen the knots in his neck and back from sleeping on the ground. He drank from the sweet crystal pool again and tried a new kind of fruit that he had found the day before. He recalled the swamp water near Gehenna and marveled once again at how far he had come since that initial misfortune. Ever since he had left that place, things had been slowly getting better and better. With any luck, that trajectory would continue.

After his foraged breakfast, Michael found the path again and continued his trek, though he had no idea what, exactly, he was walking towards. The trail looked as though it had not been walked upon by another human being for months, or perhaps longer. In the absence of walkers, it was silently fading back into the landscape. In a few more months, it would disappear entirely.

The trail climbed a steep hill, and close to the hilltop the trees parted to reveal a splendid chateau, standing tall like a miniature castle, nestled among the tall tamarisks and firs. The closer Michael drew to it, the more the land seemed to take on an aura of magic, as though everything was just a little more than reality. The perfectly random artistry of nature gave way to the subtle enhancements of meticulous tending, and then to the surreal perfection of the most gifted landscapist. The chateau also seemed to grow in size, and its salt-white marble walls shone so brightly in the morning glow that Michael was almost sure he could hear a slight hum emanating from them. Though the garden approaching the giant building was laid out like a maze, he found himself led, rather than obstructed, by the complex patterns. A giant clock tower dominated the grounds, a four-sided monolith six stories high, and like the rest of the architecture, it seemed to be cut from one single piece of white polished marble. The hands and numbers were made of black wrought iron in an ornate style reminiscent of Faberge. The word "Paradisa" had been carved deeply into the stone under each one of the clock faces. Though the words were carved in a style like old Roman lettering, the incongruity seemed particularly artful to Michael, though if he was asked to explain, he wouldn't have been able to put it into words. It was just...perfect. Like everything else on the grounds.

Everywhere he looked as he wandered the vast grounds he saw marvels: hedges cut skillfully into the shape of animals, people, and more abstract designs, beds of tulips and irises, carpets of crocuses blooming in patterns like Persian rugs, and bowers of roses surrounding the chateau. Strong, lofty walls reflected the work of superb masons. Arched doorways, domed ceilings, and galleried patios were interconnected by halls decorated with extravagant plasterwork ornamented in gold leaf and inlaid silver.

Michael's trance was interrupted by the sound of splashing water and women's laughter on the other side of a hedge wall.

Peering through the sculpture hedges, he saw a group of women swimming in a pool cut into the marble of a patio. Like everything else here, these were the most beautiful women he had ever seen. They all seemed to be devoting their attention to a grotesquely fat man who was sitting on a throne overlooking the pool. They held plates of food which he gobbled up, and handed him goblets of wine which he slurped down. The fine satin of his tunic was stained burgundy by the rivulets of drink which dribbled down his chin as he drank and from time to time he paused his feast to release a tremendous belch.

The women seemed unbothered by the man's antics, and appeared in fact to be entertained by them. They giggled and clapped when he produced flatulence with a sound like a thunderclap echoing from the marble walls. He greeted their laughter with his own, great thunderous guffaws that shook his enormous frame.

Then the man spotted Michael and his expression soured immediately. He pushed himself to his feet with a huff.

"Get out of here," he snapped at the woman, who immediately scattered and disappeared. Michael wondered as they fled, their faces still smoothed into perfect smiles, if they were really people at all, or just figments, illusions; they certainly weren't acting like any women he'd ever met.

The man motioned Michael forward and watched him suspiciously as Michael walked around the swimming pool. The closer Michael got, the more he was astonished by this man's attire. He was bedecked everywhere in elaborate jewelry, from gold bangles to gem-encrusted rings on every finger and a dozen silver pendants around his neck.

"What is this place?" Michael said. "Who are you?"

The man sat back down, shaking his head and smiling.

"Welcome to Paradisa, my fair friend," he said, waving vaguely at the grounds. "My name is H. Mortimer Snodgroot-Ralph—Mort to my friends." He drew out the final word with a slight tone of mischief to match his smile. "So what's the best your mamma could do?"

"What?" It took Michael a moment to register what he had been asked. "Oh. She named me Michael Seymour."

Mortimer stroked his chin. "And you aren't one of mine. So where in the hell did you come from?"

Michael had to stop and think for a moment. "The Altar of the Cup?" he said, not entirely sure Mortimer would understand. In response to Mortimer's blank look, Michael added, "The Holy Mountain?"

"The Holy Mountain? The Altar of the Cup? Sounds like a joke someone made up on the fly." Mortimer laughed, then started popping grapes in his mouth and tried to laugh around them, making the juice squish out of the corners of his mouth. "Have some grapes?" He extended his hand, dripping with juice.

Michael took a bushel. As soon as he popped one in his mouth, he realized how hungry he was and promptly ate the rest.

"We've got a hungry one, haven't we?" Mortimer said. Then he clapped his hands and bellowed over his shoulder, "Food! Food!"

In seconds, the group of young women came running back— or was it a new group?—and set a huge spread of food across a long row of tables quick as magic.

"Eat!" Mortimer said.

Michael wasn't about to say no. He pulled a leg off a turkey that was still steaming as though it had been taken directly from the oven. He helped himself to mounds of mashed potatoes, fresh vegetables, a piece of pie, Thanksgiving stuffing, and cranberry sauce. Everything he could think of seemed to be right there on the table—breakfast at Christmas, a Hawaiian luau, enchiladas, a Polish wedding feast.

"What, no kidney pie?" Michael joked around a mouthful of turkey.

One of the women pointed. "Right behind the leg of lamb," she said. She smiled at Michael in a way that gave him pause for a moment, though he wasn't sure why. It was like there was something...missing.

But as she'd said, sure enough, there lay a kidney pie behind the leg of lamb, like it had materialized upon his request. Michael moved from table to table, eating here and there as though he hadn't eaten in days. When he could hold no more in his stomach, he waddled over to plop himself down onto a thick pillow beside Mortimer. The man snapped his fingers and one of the women appeared with a small golden box full of aged cigars. She pulled one out, snipped a perfect cut, put it in his mouth and lit it. Violet smoke puffed upward as the man exhaled, twisting as it drifted into the eternal sky.

"Had enough already?" Mortimer said. "Anything you could possibly want is here."

"Sorry, I think I made a pig of myself," Michael said, wiping his face with an embroidered napkin.

"Michael, my man, you don't have to apologize for anything here! Paradisa will fulfill your every wish. This place is mine, created to my exact order. I can give you a few pointers on how to get your own thing going."

"Actually, Mort, I was just looking for a way to get back home," Michael said. "Can you tell me how to get out of here?"

"Out? Look around you. Why would you ever want to leave Paradisa?" Mortimer took another puff of his cigar and held up a hand. "Wait. Come and let me show you my home before you decide. Do you like my women?"

Michael blushed. He didn't know how to say what he was thinking. Women were great, fabulous actually. But he missed Wendy. Maybe, despite all his boasting, one girl was enough for him.

Mortimer analyzed Michael, scanning him up and down like Michael was a car Mort was considering buying. "Well, if you're going to stay here, you're going to need new threads at the very least, my friend."

Mortimer forced himself to stand and Michael followed suit.

"Girls!" Mort bellowed. "Clothes for...what was your name?"

"Michael."

"Clothes for Mikey!"

Five women appeared with fresh garments draped across their arms. In a matter of seconds, they disrobed Michael and clothed him in a comfortable forest green satin tunic and brown pants more comfortable than any he had ever worn. It all fit him perfectly. Once again, Michael looked around at this bizarre place in pure bewilderment. He wanted to go home, yes, but what was the rush? If Mortimer was right and this place truly offered anything Michael could ever want, he had only just scraped the surface of what was possible in Paradisa. What would be the harm in sticking around for a little while and really getting familiar with this wonderous estate? He smoothed down his tunic, marveling at how soft it was.

Mortimer stroked his beard and gazed at Michael in appreciation. "Very nice...very nice. Now that's you've been made respectable, let me show you around." He snapped his fingers and four bald men appeared, carrying an enormous sedan chair on their shoulders. All four wore only leather loincloths, and their muscular bodies gleamed with some kind of oil.

"Meet the Cadillac brothers," Mortimer said.

Their muscles rippled under the light as they knelt down and positioned the chair directly in front of Mortimer. Michael averted his eyes. As with the women, something about these men and how obediently they served Mortimer made him deeply uncomfortable. Did any of them actually want to be here, or was something more sinister at work?

Mortimer snapped his fingers again and the four silent giants lifted him off the ground and placed him into the chair. Michael jogged alongside the sedan chair, barely keeping up with the demi-gods carrying it, as Mortimer led him on an endless bragging tour of the palace.

"Do you see all these rooms? Each room will see to your every wish!"

"What do you mean, my every wish?"

"Your. Every. Wish! Which word don't you understand? Look here."

Michael's eyes widened. The room Mortimer pointed him to was covered with precious stones and jewelry. Sunlight streamed through a single window made of hundreds of panels of crystal glass. In another room, he touched life-like sculptures in awe, each one crafted from gold, diamond, and even sugar crystal.

"This is fantastic," Michael said.

"This is nothing," Mortimer said, nonchalant.

As Michael toured the chateau, he realized there were a surprising number of clocks in every room and on the grounds outside. In one hallway, a remarkable grandfather clock—around nine feet high with a massive pendulum swinging slowly—caught his eye. It seemed older than time, as though it was the first grandfather clock ever made. Michael reached out his hand to touch it.

"Don't touch the clocks!" Mortimer boomed with a sudden intensity and anxiety that surprised Michael, making him stumble back. "That is the one thing I ask," Mortimer said, his voice softening.

Michael backed away from the clock with his hands up, trying to pacify the man. "I'm sorry. I didn't know."

"I told you," Mortimer said, "there is no need for apologies here. Just look around and make yourself at home. Do whatever you want. As long as you don't touch the clocks. By tomorrow, I'm sure you'll figure out if you want to stay or not."

A gong sounded somewhere and the four coachmen opened another door and stood at attention by the chair. They moved quickly to pick up Mortimer when he signaled he was ready.

"I must attend to something," Mortimer said. "Meet me back at the pool in the morning."

"Wait, where are you going?"

"None of your concern. Look around, explore, enjoy." Then he waved a hand and the men carried him away.

No sooner had Mortimer disappeared than Mark reappeared, a worried look on his face.

"Michael, let's just get out of here. I don't have a good feeling about this place."

Michael wasn't so certain. He looked around at the lavish décor, the endless rooms full of endless wonders. "Sure, Mort's idea of a paradise is a bit...disturbing" he said. "But that doesn't mean we shouldn't give this place a chance. He was kind enough to let me stay the night, so wouldn't it be rude to just disappear without saying goodbye?"

"Michael. Will you listen to me for once in your freaking life?"

"I do listen! You won't shut up. 'Don't be an ass, Michael,' 'you're not that great, Michael,' 'you have no spirit, Michael.' Have you considered dialing back the negativity a little bit? All I've been doing is listening to you tell me how awful I am and, sure, I could be better, but can't we do just one thing that I want to do without you saying there's a problem with it? Can't there be a single moment where you're not so disappointed in me?"

Mark rolled his eyes. "Fine. If you don't want to hear from me, I won't talk anymore. I thought you were on the right path, but obviously I must have been wrong. I'm sick and tired of being your conscience."

He turned and walked away, apparently expecting to pass straight through it as he usually could. This time, however, he bumped into it and stumbled back in surprise.

"What the hell?" he said. He reached out a hand and tentatively touched the door. "I can feel it," he said, his voice low with awe. He stared at his hand and touched the doorknob, amazed to find that he could turn it and open the door. Then, as if remembering that he was angry, he opened the door the rest of the way and stormed off.

The chamber was suddenly eerily quiet. Michael could do whatever he wanted to. Mark didn't control him, and there was no way Michael would let Mark's pity party ruin what had the potential to be a very good time.

Michael turned the golden knob of a different door and stepped into a gallery filled with exquisite paintings. It took him a moment to realize that the works lining these walls were, in fact, originals. Works by Van Gogh, Da Vinci, Rockwell, Parrish, Picasso, and Pollock hung, impossibly, side by side. The engineered grotesques of H.R. Giger and Escher also made appearances, as did a matte painting on glass that no one could have done but the master Harryhausen himself. Countless other painters all had their masterpieces memorialized on the walls. Michael had never seen so many masterful works in one place. The collection on display here rivaled even the Louvre.

Strangely, three clocks of different styles—one archaic, another mid-century, the third contemporary—hung around the room, each synchronized exactly with the others, all ticking softly at the exact same time, adhering to the exact same rhythm. The concordance reminded Michael of voices synchronized in a shared chant, like the ones he had heard at the Holy Mountain. It was eerie at first but easy to forget about before long, as the steady rhythm easily slipped away from Michael's attention like a ghost.

In the middle of the room sat an easel holding an empty canvas. A palette had been freshly loaded with paints, and brushes lay on the little table just waiting to be used. Michael had never dabbled much in painting, but he felt drawn to the canvas for reasons he couldn't explain. He picked a brush up and dipped it into a pool on the palette, then almost absently started to stroke the empty canvas. The painting quickly took him away. He had no idea what he wanted to paint but seemed to discover through the act of doing. As an image began to take shape against that white canvas he realized that, yes, of course, this had been what he wanted to create all along, even if he had not consciously realized it. He laughed when he saw the image become clearer as if by magic at his touch: a portrait of a man gazing longingly at a shadow-laden desert. He knew instinctively when the painting was complete and stepped back to survey his work. It appeared less as a painting and more like a window into another world which was as real and vibrant as the room in which he now stood. It was alive!

But it was more than that. Looking from his work to the masterful canvases around the room and back again, it soon became obvious that his own piece was more deeply felt than any other painting in the room, more skillfully realized, more powerfully inspired. He marveled to imagine: if Dali or Michelangelo had been able to touch the fountain of creativity that he was experiencing, what might they have created? He had never picked up a brush before, yet in this place, he was not only able to paint, but he was able to create masterpieces beyond the reach of the greatest artists who had ever lived. He only felt a moment of doubt, quickly squashed by the evidence at hand. The strength of the work was undeniable. And if this was his first painting, imagine how exceptional he would be after ten or a hundred more!

Michael left the gallery and studio, proud of himself in a way that felt profoundly comfortable and familiar. All his life he was the best at whatever he attempted, and he embarked on new pursuits with this fact in mind, so any great achievement was only natural. But only here in Paradisa did Michael feel free enough to attempt something he had no knowledge of or experience with. Only here could he attempt things which, otherwise, would have carried the risk of failure. And it turned out he was great at these things too!

Sure, maybe it was just the magic of this place which granted him these new abilities. Or maybe it was simply because he was better at everything than he'd ever realized. He should have tried more things before. He, Michael Seymour, really was the greatest at whatever he tried to do. He'd been right to tell Mark that. Mark should have readily acknowledged the fact. It was jealousy which made Mark so angry. Simple jealousy. Mark had always been second place and he resented Michael for that fact—didn't that make more sense than any other explanation?

It was the first negative thought he'd had about his friend since Mark died. For one second, he felt ashamed. Then he wondered why he should be ashamed for simply acknowledging the truth. Wouldn't the greater disservice be to lie to himself and Mark?

Michael swaggered through the next door in the long hallway and inside he found a giant library, where the greatest words ever put to paper were shelved along the walls, with the cover of each volume's name inscribed in gold leaf: Shakespeare, Hawthorne, Heinlein, Defoe, Kozinski, Zelazny, Poe, Achebe, Ibn Battuta, Mohammad, Gandhi, Woolf, Austen, Murasaki Shikibu, Charlotte and Emily Brontë, Edith Wharton, and Zora Neale Hurston. Too many names for Michael to count. He picked up a volume of Dante and found he could read it faster than he could turn the pages. He sped through it with delight, volume after volume, until the chiming of a dozen clocks distracted him. He glanced at his wrist for a watch that wasn't there, then saw all the other clocks read six o'clock. How long had he been there?

He stood and prepared to leave when an elegant silver type-writer caught his eye. It sat on a writing desk in the middle of the room. Still flushed with excitement by the power of the painting he had just created, Michael sat down before the typewriter, set his fingers gently on the cold keys, and started to type. At first, he recoiled from the loud clack of the type bars against the platen, but after a couple more strokes of the letters flying against the paper, his fingers found themselves comfortably working the keys, as if he had been a typist in a previous life and was only now recalling the muscle memory still lodged somewhere in his brain. A tantalizing first line laid itself across the paper casually, but when he read it, his breath caught in the back of his throat. Already it was a story that no one could put down.

The hours passed swiftly as Michael wrote. Each paragraph was so eloquently designed, the drama so intense that he found himself in tears again and again. He felt like he had entered yet another world, one where he was obsessed with an intensity he was sure no drug could match. It was so much more than his transcendent running experience in the ever-changing world near the waterfall. Adrenaline flowed through his veins like an electric charge as he typed madly on, unable to free himself from the compelling story.

At last, he fell back, exhausted, and realized he had created a literary masterpiece above all other writers. No one had written like he had, not the scholars of Oxford, the masters of Rome, nor the scribes of Osiris. He ran through the stacks to the shelf, look-ing for his book, which he knew would already be on the shelves. He pulled out a handsome volume, bound in fine leather and gold, and saw his own name on the binder: Michael Seymour. He had never written an original word before, but there and then in Paradisa he was immortalized in paper and ink. He flipped open the book to the first page and found the very words he had just written.

Michael walked to the next room in a daze.

There was a giant gymnasium that was prepared for an Olympiad, with a trampoline, vaulting horses, parallel bars, rings and all the other equipment necessary for world-class competition. Though art and literary creations were new to him, Michael had been an athlete for a long time and knew these events well. He found a pair of gymnast pants and a compression shirt folded neatly on the top of a bench. Coincidentally they were his school colors, and again, coincidentally of course, the name "Seymour" appeared on the back of the compression shirt.

He changed into the uniform, feeling a little more limber once he had put it on. Then he stepped eagerly to the parallel bars, stood between them and lifted himself up. At first, his body felt somewhat stiff. Then, as he swung back and forth, he loosened up until every muscle in his body felt agile. Strength poured through him as he discovered coordination and control beyond even what he had been capable of at home. He felt indestructible, able to perform acrobatic feats as if he had been practicing for years. His body was able to endure the most extreme stress as he flew back and forth on the bar. He performed a crisp double-twisting-flip dismount and landed precisely on the pad.

He hadn't even broken a sweat.

Vowing he would return to defy the laws of gravity and the limits of art in motion, he changed back to his tunic and left the room, filled with energy and strength.

He opened the next door. Though he was certain night had just been approaching, he found a sunlit conservatory. Under its high glass panes lay an array of musical instruments. Mark was in the center, playing his guitar. A small crowd of people were listening in rapture. It was a soft melody, full of emotion and wonder and hurt that Michael could physically feel. Mark played to the end of his song and the small circle clapped emphatically, tears running down their faces.

Michael started clapping, slightly in awe over what his friend was able to create. It was amazing, though everything made in Paradisa was amazing. The small crowd vanished in a puff of violet smoke. Mark turned to Michael, stood up, and walked away. He didn't even glance Michael's way as he slipped through a door in the back corner of the room.

Michael scoffed at his friend's rudeness. Fine. He would just play something that was even better. Though something about the ornately carved harpsichord drew his attention, Michael picked up a gleaming white Gibson electric guitar. He had always secretly admired Mark's knack for picking out tunes with such ease. He owed it to his friend to at least try it, at least find an appreciation for being the player, the entertainer. Besides, there was nobody else in the room to laugh at him, or to dictate how and what he played. He didn't have to appease others. He could just focus on what he himself liked.

As before, sitting and seating the guitar in his lap felt familiar, automatic. His thumb found its way to the center of the neck and his fingers curled easily around to pluck the strings. He could intuitively feel just where he should put his fingers to form the chords. He softly stroked the strings and then plucked them with an increasing confidence, the sound of music filling the chamber, reverberating with the classical touch of a professional. As he played, Michael laughed to recall Mortimer's words. "Each room will see to your every wish." This was a wish he hadn't even known he had, yet still the room made it real for him. Could this place read his mind? Even parts of his mind he didn't know were there?

The music took him away. He knew what it meant to be a genius and a master, able to evoke any song he could hear in his mind. His hands simply did as they pleased and he received the most sublime of sounds from the strings. Tears rolled down his cheeks and for the first time, he felt he really understood what music was; it was not an earthly gift, but some magic, straight from heaven, which spoke directly to the soul.

On a sudden impulse, he put the guitar back and ran to the huge grand piano which dominated the room. His hands leapt to the keys and he started to play. The piano came alive at his touch and his mind and heart fell deep into the music. Then, when he thought there could be no greater sound, a curtain swept back from one wall, revealing a high proscenium behind which sat a full symphonic orchestra. Its full chords filled the room with acoustic perfection as the musicians picked up the theme he had created and wove a rhapsody around his brilliant statements, his eloquent counter-points. Like a man in the throes of deepest passion, he played, and after a crescendo to a coda like the rising of Asgard from the flames, he collapsed onto the keyboard, exhausted.

He then heard the roar of the audience as another curtain, opposite the proscenium, pulled back to reveal the source of the deep-throated cheers and screams of the people taken to heights beyond themselves.

"Bravo! Bravo!" they cried, tears streaming down their cheeks.

Their presence startled him. Suddenly embarrassed, he held out his hands apologetically.

"Look, I really don't know how to do this. I've never touched a piano before."

In an instant, the curtains flew across the wall, the crowd and the orchestra disappeared, and Michael was alone in the still chamber. The sudden, total silence was so complete that for a split second, Michael wondered if he'd gone deaf, somehow, until he heard the sound of his own heartbeat in his ears.

He sat a moment to catch his breath, but then he thought he heard someone moving close by. "Is anybody there?" he said.

He heard no reply, nothing but the soft ticking of a lonely clock.

Chapter 11

After another moment of quiet, Michael became certain that he wasn't alone.

"Hello?" he said again.

"Yes, Michael?" The voice behind him, though gentle, made him jump.

He turned to see a young woman standing in the doorway. She was dressed in the same clothes Wendy had worn the last time he saw her. In fact, she sort of looked like Wendy, except a photoshopped version, as if someone had gone through with a brush and removed every blemish. There was a strange feeling of unreality about her. "Flawless" was the only word Michael could think of, and he wasn't sure that was such a good thing.

"You could probably use a break after everything you've been up to today," she said.

Why did she have to look so much like Wendy? He found his thoughts pulled back to his last conversation with her, the pain he had felt standing alone and defeated in front of her house. He tried to focus and keep himself in the present.

"What's your name?" he said.

"What would you like my name to be?"

He shrugged. *Wendy* was in his head and on the tip of his tongue but he didn't say it.

"Then I'm Mindy," she said.

He laughed. It was almost like she'd read his mind but hadn't quite got it right.

"What a great name," he said.

She brightened. "We've got this really nice steam room just through that door. I'm sure you could use a bit of heat to loosen up."

She led him to the sauna, where he found a towel waiting for him.

Mindy averted her gaze as he undressed and wrapped the towel around his waist, then they stepped into the steam-filled room. Mindy opted not to change, though her clothes were ill-suited for so much heat and humidity. It seemed to not even occur to her that this might be strange.

"The steam will help relax your muscles," she said from across the room, half-obscured by vapor. "You certainly deserve it after that riveting performance in the gymnasium."

Something about Mindy's tone seemed...off. But for the moment, Michael decided he felt too relaxed to care. And it was nice to be complimented.

"You saw my performance?"

"Of course," she said with a smile. "It was televised."

Michael couldn't keep from smiling. The thought of being broadcast in all his victorious glory after that complete mess of a race he had just lost was a source of triumph and vindication. How long ago had that race happened, anyway? It seemed like a thousand centuries ago now.

"Every wonderful thing you've been doing since you got to Paradisa has been televised," Mindy said.

"Everything?" Were there tiny cameras all over this place? Did they have the same cameras in the bathroom? Were they filming him right now? He decided not to think about it. The whole idea was a little unsettling. Surely there was privacy in this world, if he wished for it.

"The sauna is also very good for detoxing," Mindy said. "You can't imagine how much toxicity even the healthiest of people can accumulate in their bodies. But, boy, it sure is hot in here."

The mist cleared long enough for Michael to see Mindy's face clearly. He tongue was hanging against her bottom lip and she was painting with quick, rapid breaths.

Michael's confusion must have shown on his face because Mindy quickly retracted her tongue and smiled broadly.

"Oh, excuse me," she said. "How un-lady like."

They sat in silence for a few moments, just breathing. Every

JOURNEY OF THE SPIRIT MAN

breath Michael drew was longer and deeper and he found himself sinking into a relaxed state more profound than any he had ever experienced. Despite the heat, he felt he could probably stay here until he melted into a puddle and wouldn't mind at all.

"Isn't this nice?" Mindy said.

"Yeah, it's a real treat."

"Did you say treat?" Mindy sat up, smiled and panted, excited.

Michael blinked at her, uncomfortable. Something peculiar was going on. A burst of steam clouded his vision and he could no longer see her. The steam slowly cleared.

"Michael?" she sounded concerned. "You look flushed. Let me take a look at you." She glided across the steam room to sit beside him.

Up close, she looked more familiar than before. Had her features changed slightly, or was he just imagining that? Hair a little darker, nose a little longer, a barely-perceptible squint around her eyes. She looked exactly like Wendy now—so much so that Michael blurted her name without thinking.

"Wendy?" he said.

"Yes?"

She didn't seem to notice or care that he had called her the wrong name. Who was this person? Was it possible she had really become Wendy? Paradisa was supposed to grant his every wish, after all, and reuniting with Wendy had definitely been near the front of his mind for most of his stay here.

Was it Wendy? His brain felt fuzzy. He couldn't remember exactly how he got here, and even as he grasped at his memories, the name Mindy faded into nothing but steam. The woman sitting next to him had always been named Wendy—of course she had. But Michael couldn't be certain that she was the Wendy he knew because he couldn't remember anything about Wendy, her personality, the things that made her who she was. What were her hobbies? What was her major? What did she do when she wasn't with him? The steam filled his lungs as he took a deep breath, the answers to his questions slipping further from him than ever.

"I still love you, Michael," Wendy said. "I've always loved you."

"I'm sorry, Wendy," he said. "I'm sorry for what I said to you at the race. I'm sorry I wasn't better to you."

"Shhh," she said. "Shhh." She put a finger on his lips.

"I love you too, Wendy," he said.

Wendy leaned in and Michael found himself leaning towards her as well. Their lips drew close together as a cocktail of endorphins flooded his brain. But then, instead of kissing him as he expected, she stuck out her tongue and licked the side of his face. He jerked back, baffled, and she just stared at him expectantly, panting, with her tongue lolling out of the side of her mouth.

"Wendy, what was that about?"

"Tell me, Michael" she said. "Do you like dogs?"

He shook his head, trying to escape the mental fog that had settled over him. This wasn't Wendy. Who was she again? Mindy. Right. Mindy, not Wendy. He took a step back. He didn't want to be here. He didn't want to be doing this. A sudden wave of nausea accompanied by a new sub-spinal sensation came over him, as he saw, rising over his right shoulder, his own tail.

What was happening to him? Was he...was he becoming a...?

Michael jumped from his sleep, gasping for air. He swiveled left and right, agitated, the down duvet sliding down around his waist. He didn't remember falling asleep, but he must have, at some point. Maybe after his solo on the piano? And someone must have carried him to this bed without waking him. He thought of the muscular men who carried Mortimer wherever he wanted to go and felt a twinge of embarrassment at the idea that he had inadvertently forced them to carry him, too.

It was still dark outside, but any thought of sleep had been murdered. He thought about the steam room and the strangeness of it all. Yet, at the same time, everything had been so vivid, so real. Was it really only a dream?

He rubbed his tailbone. No tail. That was a relief. Still, he felt like he'd had quite enough of this estate for the time being. Though there were hours of night left to go, he stayed in bed until daybreak, fearing what might happen if he walked the magical halls in the dark. As the sunrise filtered into his bedchamber, Michael rubbed his eyes and checked around the room once more to ensure he was alone. He got out of bed and gazed out a window that looked out across the high mountain range. Here in this uncertain place, with the bizarre dream close on his heels, he missed Wendy more than anything.

Michael ran his fingers through his neatly trimmed hair and stroked his cleanshaven face, wondering only for a second when he had visited a barber between yesterday and today. But such questions were pointless in a place like Paradisa.

"All right, Michael," he said to himself. "What wonders are you going to perform today?" He was a bit surprised to hear the sarcasm in his voice. He really *could* perform wonders here, so what was the problem? Well, aside from the uneasy dreams.

A chime sounded, and bells, and then from everywhere the sound of clocks chiming on the hour. His meeting with Mortimer was close at hand, and he began to suspect there was an unwelcome truth awaiting him there. New clothes hung on a bedside valet, and a pair of new tennis shoes stood beside the bed, waiting to be worn. They were exactly like the pair he had at home, only they were brand new.

Michael walked down the hallway to a central court, where he found Mortimer sitting on his throne, smoking a cigar. The man grinned as he saw Michael approach.

"I take it you have enjoyed your stay so far. Am I correct?"

Michael sat down on a small stool beside Mortimer and helped himself to a Bavarian-cream-loaded Bismarck. "I had the strangest dream last night..." he said, but trailed off as Mortimer began to smile expectantly. After a long pause, Michael said, "What are you doing here, Mortimer?"

Mortimer frowned. "Have a cup of coffee."

Michael accepted a porcelain cup of the finest and freshest coffee he had ever tasted.

"Paradisa is here to satisfy me, to take care of me," Mortimer said, lighting another cigar.

"What good is a place where everything you want can be easily attained? Where every wish and every thought can come true simply by thinking about it?" Michael said. For some reason, he hadn't considered this before. He'd been so busy enjoying what Paradisa had to offer that he didn't stop to think about what it meant to consume thoughtlessly. Only as the words leapt from his lips did he realize how true they were.

Mortimer sipped his coffee. "Isn't that what everybody lives for? So they can die and come here? There is no disease, no pain, no suffering."

"No goals, no hope, no success," Michael countered. "How can you stay here?"

"How can you even think of leaving here?"

"This world is without substance, without striving, without meaning!" The words came from somewhere inside Michael, though he wasn't sure where. God, he sounded like Mark.

"I am a god here," Mortimer said. "I *am* the meaning. I *am* the substance."

Michael blew on his coffee, forgetting it was already the perfect temperature, and took a small sip. "A god of what, Mort? Artificial perfection? There's no point to this place, it's completely self-serving."

Michael had always hated the idea of serving anybody else, but in reality, didn't he serve the spectators in the stands every time he won a race? Did he not receive glory for something that came effortlessly to him? And yet he reveled in self-satisfaction, as though he was so great, without even working for the rewards he received.

Mortimer said nothing for a moment, but when Michael glanced up and looked into his eyes, he saw the man's pain. "People have made fun of me, abused me, tried to cheat me, ignored me, and acted like I was stupid. No matter how hard I tried to be a good man, people have never taken me seriously. I started hating everyone, including myself." He shook his head sadly. "Don't you see? No one makes fun of me here. No one abuses me. No one ignores me. More than that, everyone here loves me!"

"Yeah, I understand," Michael said, "but you're still alone."

Mortimer didn't answer.

"Thanks for the coffee, Mort. And the hospitality. But I've got to try and find my way back home."

"Wait," Mortimer grasped Michael's arm. "There is still one thing that I want to show you. It's the best part of Paradisa."

"Really, I just need to get going," Michael said.

"Just one more thing," Mortimer begged. "Trust me, you simply must see this."

Michael looked towards the mountain and sighed. He had to admit he wasn't exactly on a schedule. "OK, show me what you want to show me."

Mortimer got up from the table and Michael followed him to one of several arched steel doorways, which led into the base of the tall marble clock tower. Mortimer pulled the doors wide but still the space inside remained so dark Michael could barely see anything within it.

"What are you going to show me?" Michael said.

"The truth, Michael—what this place is really all about." The words send a chill down Michael's spine. He felt a sense of vindication, as well. Of *course* there was more at work here than met the eye, just as he had suspected. Mortimer stood aside and Michael stepped into the dimly lit clocktower.

"You're right, Michael," Mortimer said from the doorway. "Even in my own paradise, I am alone. The longing for real companionship here, for someone real to share this wonderful place with, has always gone unfulfilled. That is why I can't let you go." With that, he stepped back with surprising speed and swung the heavy door shut. A booming thud sounded throughout the room as he dropped a heavy metal bar into place on the opposite side, trapping Michael within.

"Mortimer!" Michael shouted. He pounded on the door. "Mortimer!"

"I'm sorry, Michael," came the muffled voice from the other side. "I truly am. But I cannot be alone again."

Michael searched for a handle that wasn't there. "You don't have to be," he said. "You could come with me."

"Oh, dear. I had hoped you would understand. I can't go back into the world outside. This place is everything to me and it could be everything to you, too. But everyone who comes here ends up leaving—and why? Why seek dissatisfaction when they could have fulfillment, why pursue things they cannot have when they could have everything? I know you must be angry with me right now, but you'll change your mind after you think about it for a while."

"Mortimer, wait!" Michael called, but Mortimer's heavy footsteps receded and before long they were gone. Michael was left in dark silence with no way out.

Eventually, his eyes adjusted enough to the lack of light that he spotted a dim glow emanating from a vertical crack in the wall. It was far too narrow to escape through, and barely allowed a sliver of a view of the grounds outside when he pressed his eye up to it. He felt his way around the room, hoping to stumble across something which might help him in some way, but the room was completely bare. What was the point of this place if it was entirely empty? Shouldn't there at least be tools or something in here?

As if on cue, he stumbled over something he could have sworn hadn't been there a moment ago: a large chisel and mallet. He sighed. It was something, but the thought of chipping through a foot or two of solid marble wasn't his idea of a good time. Still, it was all he had, so he picked up the tools, placed the chisel against the crack in the wall, and prepared to start chipping.

Just before he brought the hammer down, however, Mortimer appeared outside, shouting his name.

"Michael! Michael!"

Michael leaned closer to the crack and saw that Mortimer stood next to one of the men who carried his sedan chair.

"Look, Michael," Mortimer said. "Can you do this in your world and still be loved?" With the back of his hand, he struck the man across the face, leaving an angry red mark on his cheek. Recovering his balance, the man turned to him and apologized for whatever he had done to anger Mortimer.

"Do you see?" Mortimer said. He slapped the man again and said, "Kiss my feet!"

The man knelt and did as he was asked without complaint.

"It's Paradisa, after all," Mortimer said. "You can do no wrong in Paradisa. All is forgiven in Paradisa, Michael. Don't you have plenty of things you'd like to be forgiven for?" He waited for a response for some time, and when Michael offered none, he turned and left in a huff. A moment later, the bald man stood and followed after him.

Michael shook his head. Yamani's words came back to him: *Not every nexus of evil is as blatant as Gehenna.* Paradisa had become a hell for everyone in it—including Mortimer. He turned his attention back to the wall, then changed his mind. Rather than chipping a way out, he went to the opposite wall, which would lead toward the main clocktower chamber. Somehow, he felt certain that going toward the center of the tower would help him find his ticket out of this nightmare. Holding the chisel steady, Michael brought the hammer down with grace and strength he had previously believed impossible. A large piece of marble broke off immediately, then another. It was exhilarating work, not the drudgery he had expected, and a surge of energy shot through him. He was wild with adrenaline as his arm flew back and forth, breaking off piece after piece, until a chunk so large broke from the wall and he could simply step through to the other side.

Looking back, he saw he had actually cut a perfectly rectangular doorway from the other room. It was a magnificent piece of craftsmanship, with the most perfect of angles that not even the most expert of surveyors could—

"Oh, give me a break," Michael muttered.

Beyond the hole in the wall rose a spiral staircase, also carved from a single block of marble. Michael could only assume it led to the top of the tower, where the giant clock was. Given Mortimer's anxiety when Michael had nearly touched one of the smaller clocks, he imagined something up there could give him the upper hand, though he had no idea yet what it might be. As he climbed the staircase, hundreds of pigeons flew from perches around the inside of the tower, frightened by the echoing footsteps. Fluttering and screeching, they flung themselves along the walls, struggling to escape through a small opening at the very top of the building.

When Michael finally reached the top, he entered the clock room through a large iron door. The timepiece had looked impressive from the outside, but it was even more striking from in here, where he could see all the gears which made it tick. It looked like it might have been the oldest mechanical clock in the world. Each piece, each cogwheel, ratchet, and lever bore the marks of hand filing, preening, and polishing. Each cogwheel from the largest to the tiniest turned rhythmically second by second, driven by chained weights and a long pendulum tipped with a polished sphere a foot across.

Michael listened to the cooing of the pigeons as they found their way back to their perches, and to the interminable, implacable chik-kachung, chik-kachung of the clock. Unstoppable.

Michael stared at the relentless mechanism and he understood Mortimer's misery. If there was such a place as heaven, surely it would be eternal. But in the illusion of Paradisa, time was still running out. Even though every form of human accomplishment seemed possible, it was still, in some very important sense, done on borrowed time.

Small gears and cogwheels turned to the seconds, medium sprockets turned to the minutes, and the ponderous pendulum slowly swung back and forth, measuring each chik-kachung of the escape wheel. Michael took the heavy iron bar which he guessed was intended to bar the door, and he tried to jam it into the teeth of the sprockets. But no matter how he levered the bar, he could not stop or even slow down the clock.

The pendulum had an adjustment device on it, a screw-like thread on which the sphere could be turned to move it up and down on its long shaft. Somewhere in the back of his mind, Michael recalled learning that a pendulum's period, the time it takes to swing back and forth, is not determined by how far back and forth it swings, but by how long the pendulum is. This one had been turned all the way down to the bottom, so it was measuring time as slowly as it possibly could. Michael twirled the sphere and the weight gradually climbed higher and higher along the arm. As it rose, the pendulum swung faster and faster and the ticking of the clock accelerated exponentially.

Michael gave the sphere one final spin and the clock tower seemed to come alive. The large cogwheel spun and the giant apparatus churned like a metallic monster. Hours began to chime almost constantly, and he was sure he could smell lubricating oil heating up as the gears moved reached a feverish speed.

And it wasn't just the clock which moved faster. Michael peered out the window and saw everything accelerating. The sun and moon zipped alternatingly across the sky. No sooner had the sun appeared on the eastern horizon than it disappeared into the west. Day and night and day and night flickered in and out at a nauseating pace. From below, Michael heard Mortimer wail.

"How much time do you have left, Mortimer?" he shouted.

Mortimer appeared from the chateau. "How did you...Put it back! Please, put the clock back!" There was so much anguish in his voice that Michael almost felt sorry for him. Almost.

In a few short minute-hours, Mortimer raced to the tower and flung open the door, his face pale and sagging. His hair had grown considerably, his snout was beginning to turn up, and two little tusks were developing under both sides of his upper lip.

"Please! Stop!" he snorted, shuddering as he tried to catch his breath.

Michael stood staring at him, truly shocked by his inhuman appearance. Finally, he relented, and spun the sphere back to where it had begun. The pendulum's weight sank back down and time resumed its usual crawling pace.

"You are free to leave," Mortimer said, resigned. "It was a desperate move, I admit it. I was wrong to try to keep you here."

"Why do you stay here? Look at what you've become."

"I hate being lonely, but I would rather be lonely than face the humiliation I faced in the world." Mortimer sank to the floor, covering his face with his hands, and he began to blubber and bawl.

"Let me tell you something," Michael said. "I was like you. I thought I had nothing. My whole life fell apart right in front of my eyes and everyone I cared about abandoned me or died. But this?" He gestured to the grounds of Paradisa, the beautiful hedges and the pristine estate. "This isn't the answer. You can't just force the world to bow to your every whim. You're the one who's gotta change." He put his hand on Mortimer's shoulder for a moment, then stepped around him towards the door. "I hope you find the courage to get out of this candy-coated hell."

He walked down the staircase to the bottom of the tower, flung open the door, and marched to the main hall. He walked as though he knew exactly where he was going, because somehow he did. He finally stopped before a modest door, one without gold trim or a ruby-inlaid handle. Mortimer, who had tagged along meekly, kept his distance from the door, as if he didn't recognize it and didn't trust it.

"What's in there?" he said.

Michael smiled. "My every wish, remember?"

He opened the door. Rather than leading to another room full of indescribable wonders, this door led back outside the chateau. The forest path down which Michael had traveled to get here was no longer quite so lush as it had been, nor did the trees sport countless impossible blooms. But there was something comforting about such a mundane scene after so much time spent in this magically altered prison. Mortimer looked at the door, then looked at Michael uncertainly.

"Come with me," Michael said. "It's not too late."

Michael nudged the door open a little wider. Then, without waiting for a response, he stepped through. A moment later, Mortimer appeared at his side and took a deep breath.

"The air is so much fresher out here," he marveled. "It's so easy to breathe!"

"You should see why." Michael motioned to the natural pool beneath the waterfall where, not so long ago, he had bathed and basked in the sun. Mort stood at the pool's edge and touched his hands to his face to be sure that what he was seeing was real. There he stood, a middle aged pudgy man, with a wide nose and a comb-over, dressed in a maroon collared shirt, tan slacks, and brown loafers. Nothing like the grotesque caricature of a man he'd been when Michael first arrived.

"My Lord," he said. "I look just like I did the day I arrived here! You did this for me?"

"Consider it a second opportunity," Michael said. He was relieved to see that his own appearance hadn't changed. Well, except for one addition: his ring. He twisted it automatically like he always did when he needed a boost of luck, a wide grin on his face. He stared at the ring, appreciating every moment he'd gone through without it, and silently vowed he would continue to be the person he had claimed his ring gave him the power to be. He would still be exceptional, of course. But this time, his talents would be accompanied by humility and compassion for others. And he'd somehow find the courage to risk trying new things, things he might not be so good at, at least at first, but would enjoy doing anyway. Like painting. Or music.

Michael found the path and prepared to follow it wherever it took him next. He looked over his shoulder and saw Mortimer standing amid the trees, a little confused and afraid.

"Where should I go?" Mortimer said. "I don't know where to go."

"Just start walking," Michael said. "You'll find your own path along the way." Then he turned and strolled into the thick forest, leaving Mortimer to find his own way. He wondered if he would ever see the man again, but even as he thought that, he knew he would not.

After a short while, Michael sensed Mark's presence beside him. The two strolled in silence for a time, neither one feeling the need to acknowledge the other. The anger that had simmered between them before felt useless now, childish. It was Mark who finally broke the silence.

"I get it," he said. "Maybe not entirely, but... I understand better now."

"Understand what?"

"What it feels like to be the best at something, and why that's so... intoxicating. When I was back there, when I could be the best in the world at anything I tried...Well, I'd be lying if I said I didn't consider staying. So I get why it's hard to give all that up."

Michael nodded. "You were right, though. Again. There's always a price."

They walked another mile without speaking, both lost in thought and simply appreciating the simple pleasure of the natural world around them.

"Why do you stick with me?" Michael said at last. "I don't listen to you, I make you furious, so why do you still follow me everywhere?"

"I don't have a choice," Mark said. "I can't leave. Ever since Gehenna, I've been dragged along with your sorry ass wherever you go." Mark squinted up at the sky. "Sometimes I wonder if I ever really left Gehenna. It's where I belong. I failed you."

"You didn't. You saved my life and I just wish I could have done the same for you. You're my best friend, man."

Tears sprung to Mark's eyes. "You are too, Michael. You drive me crazy but you are too. Do you have any idea how much I want to go back to when we were kids and we did everything for fun? That's what I found in Paradisa—a place where we were kids again and... I wasn't dead."

So there it was. It had been real before Mark said it, of course, but the words themselves made it undeniable. He was dead, and nothing Michael could do was going to change that. Up to this point, Mark seemed so cool, so on top of everything. It seemed like he didn't really care if he was dead or not. But it was obvious now he had been hiding his true feelings. Mark was scared. He had spent so much of his time helping Michael, and Michael hadn't even noticed the pain he was in.

Michael put his hand on Mark's shoulder but he phased right

through it. Mark had only been corporeal in Paradisa.

"I don't know what to say," Michael said. "Tell me what you need and I'll do it."

Mark shook his head. "That's not for me to decide. This path we're on right now is yours. I'm just along for the ride."

"I just want to go home," Michael said.

Mark smiled. "I know. But you know what you did back there in Paradisa? You've grown a lot. I'd say you're definitely headed in the right direction."

"I don't know," Michael said. "I hope so."

Mark nodded at the path ahead. "Let's keep going, then, Spirit Man. Let's go home."

Chapter 12

Michael trekked through the forest with a new kind of confidence. With Paradisa behind him, he felt certain that his trials were nearing an end. Sooner or later, this path had to take him back home. Back to the real world. But he no longer dreamed of going "back to normal." His life had changed, after all, and he wasn't going to try to fight that change anymore. He'd have to figure out what it meant to live with his life-altering disease, and what his future would be without the Olympics. He'd have to salvage what remained of his relationships and find ways to help them flourish.

But there would be time for all of that later. Right now, he just had to figure out how to get home. *Home.* The word echoed in his head. Never had a word sounded better. Home might not be perfect but it was the only place he belonged.

Somewhere along the way, Mark disappeared again. What was with that guy and vanishing right when Michael thought he would get some actual continuous company? Overhead, low menacing clouds began to gather, and thunder echoed off the hills as lightning lit the forest. The clouds turned a darker gray and scuttled across the sky like lost souls, growing more and more restless, more and more tattered.

The sky darkened further as the sounds of thunder grew louder. Soon, ragged sheets of rain fell across the mountainside not far ahead. As the first drops began to splatter the path around Michael, he came to a large crevice in the rock face beside him. How convenient.

He ducked into the chamber to seek shelter from the advancing storm. The cave widened inside, allowing more than enough room for him to fit, though it may not have been the most comfortable of places. The light coming in through the crevice was meager, but

JOURNEY OF THE SPIRIT MAN

offered a glimpse of the cavern beyond his shelter, which plunged down into blackness. He had no sense of how big the space truly was, and he wasn't sure he wanted to find out. Stuck between the cavern and the growing rainstorm, he found his thoughts returning again and again to what might be lingering there in the dark.

"I wish I could have some lights in here," he said, hoping the magic of Paradisa might stretch a little beyond the Chateau. When the darkness of the cave stared back at him, unblinking, Michael sighed, though he had to admit he was only slightly disappointed. Paradisa was definitely behind him.

A tremendous thunderclap shook the crevice, followed by another. It sounded as if the mountain was splitting apart. White-hot flashes of lightning stabbed across the sky, bright enough to illuminate the little cleft so brightly it almost hurt, and making the shadows even darker when they returned. As the wind grew fiercer, it rushed over the crevice as over the aperture of a whistle, producing a deep vibration from the cave. The rock faces trembled with the sound, and Michael worried his shelter might collapse on him without warning.

He crept close to the edge of the opening so he could peer out. The valley was in constant motion, like the dangerous waters of a storm-swept sea. The rain raked the land in wind-torn ragged sheets, the trees bent nearly to their breaking points as the gusts stripped them of leaves. The valley itself had flooded entirely and streams of muddy water cut dark channels through the soil in their tumbling rush to reach the canyon below. One such stream had begun flowing into the cave in which Michael hid and was growing with alarming speed. Turning, he saw that water was filling the lower portion of the chamber, rising higher by the second. If the rain didn't stop soon, he would have to either brave the storm outside or drown in the cave.

The moment came before he was ready. In a flash, the water filling the cave's basin reached his feet, then his ankles. He couldn't shake the feeling that this was happening for a reason. The water, like the path in the desert at the beginning of his journey, was urging him onward. He was not meant to wait out this storm, he was meant to step into the torrent and do all that he could to stay above water. He wasn't sure if this thought was comforting or disturbing, but he didn't have much time to ponder it. It was time to go.

Michael braced himself against the rocks and stepped out of the cave. The fierce rain struck him like whirling fists, stinging and numbing his face. He was immediately soaked. He felt like he was wearing cement shoes. The noise alone was equally awe inspiring and terrifying; if he screamed he would not even hear it.

He crouched against the rock face and clung to a narrow crack to keep from being swept away. The wind, already hurricane strength, picked up even further. As he watched, trees and shrubs across the valley were fully uprooted and sent careening toward the canyon. Then a powerful gust struck Michael directly and he lost his grip. It plucked him from the rock face like a doll and sent him tumbling and sliding in the slick mud toward the largest of the developing arroyos. Just as he thought he was inescapably doomed, the wind slammed him against the trunk of a splintered tree. He grabbed the stump with both arms and pulled himself up to wrap his legs around it. For a moment, he was a lone static point amid the gale, an immovable anchor surrounded by storm-wracked seas. But the moment didn't last.

A rumble from above signaled the arrival of a six-foot wall of mud plunging down the slope towards him. He didn't even have time to react before the wall slammed into him, wrenched him from the log, and flung him once more into the dark swirling mass. He was sucked under immediately and began swimming with the current to stay somewhat afloat, grasping desperately for anything sturdy.

Then, it was all over; he felt himself suddenly falling free and knew he had been spit out over the edge of a cliff. He submitted himself to the inevitable death he knew would come when he reached the bottom of whatever it was that he had fallen from. His acceptance of this fact surprised him, but he realized he still wasn't sure if he had been alive or dead during this entire strange journey, so who could say what would happen when he hit the ground? He took one last deep breath and waited for the end.

Michael awoke spitting out a mouthful of mud. A wave of deep nausea swept over him and he retched up another gush of muddy water, then lay there on the edge of consciousness waiting for the spinning to stop. In a vague and dreamlike way, he realized that once again, miraculously, he had survived.

The sound of thunder drifted off as the storm went on to torment some other valley, and soon Michael felt sunlight warming his back. He thought he could hear a waterfall some distance away and wondered if that was where he had fallen. Raising himself up to look around was out of the question in his current battered state, so all he could do was muse at his unlikely circumstances. Through the haze he began to hear voices over the rushing water.

"Over here," someone said. "He's alive!"

With great effort, Michael opened one eye and looked up to see four men in ancient Egyptian armor staring at him. One of the men prodded him roughly with a sandaled toe, and another drew his sword.

"We will take him to En-Ausar Simbel."

When they grasped him by the shoulders and hauled him to his feet, he was surprised to discover he was completely naked. They wasted no time in whipping him with short little quirts, as though they were accustomed to find people lying naked by the river.

"What the hell?" Michael said, the pain snapping him out of his half-conscious stupor.

"Get moving," one of the men ordered. He kicked Michael in the rear.

Michael staggered ahead. The men ushered him along a winding path through golden dunes and past fields of grain and rows of date palm trees. Were it not for the rather unfriendly company, the walk would have been quite a pleasant one. At last, they came to a wide, slow moving river, along which were perched numerous mud brick buildings. The men led Michael to a low building which appeared to be a barracks of some kind, not unlike the adobe worker's quarters he knew back in New Mexico. Inside the walled compound, he saw hundreds of workers—slaves, judging by the way they were treated—being herded about by a cadre of men in loincloths and trapezoidal headgear. One among them was clearly the master of all. She wore a robe embroidered with gold thread, and had several well-oiled servants and jeweled handmaidens clustered about, waiting for her word. Michael's captors threw Michael headlong into the dust before her.

"We found this by the river, beneath Cheron's Fall, Lady Simbel," his captor said.

Lady Simbel looked Michael over and wrinkled up her face. "What god do you serve?" she said.

Michael frowned. "I...I guess I don't serve any particular god."

"A man with no god? Then you are certainly not from here. What are you called?"

"I'm Michael Seymour," he said wearily. "I came from...the other side of the mountains. There was a storm."

"We saw the storm," she said loftily. "It was very unusual. These are the rains that heal our land from year to year, but never before have we seen such a vicious storm that could tear away even the face of the mountains."

Michael glanced over at the mountain. It had indeed been heavily eroded within the last few hours. It looked like it had experienced an explosion. If the storm had done all of *that*, he had no idea how he himself could have survived such a cataclysm.

The noblewoman turned to address the leader of the patrol. "There is something very significant about this slave's arrival. A man without a god...I must consult the oracles to discover just what that may mean. You will take him to the monastery and see that he is properly prepared for my audience."

Michael wanted to ask if everyone was speaking English, but he figured the answer would be similar to the one Yamani had given him. Somehow, he was able to fluently speak and understand languages he had never studied in his life. But whatever language they were speaking, it just sounded like English to him.

"So we're in Egypt?" Michael said.

Lady Simbel snorted. "Please, do not mangle the name of our mighty land on your clumsy tongue. This is Aegypt, the most modern and forward-thinking civilization in the world, thanks to the vision and will of the Most High Pharaoh, Cheron-Rey-Neteru, the destroyer of death."

"The destroyer of death?"

She gestured to the men with whips. "I'm tired of his questions. Take him away."

The men led Michael to his new quarters in one wing of the great temple palace of Cheron, on the bank of the Ciceron, the mother of rivers. It was a clean and simple room with a bed, a small table, and little else. He was cleaned, fed, and left to sleep off the exhaustion from the eventful day. The following day, his new routine began.

Each day he was awakened by silent monks and taken to the roof to greet the sunrise and give thanks to the sun god Rey. Afterward, he was taken to Simbel for tutoring in the ways of their kingdom and the gods they worshipped. It was quite an adjustment, but Michael found the strict routine comforting, in a way, especially after the overwhelming freedom of Paradisa. For the first time since arriving in this peculiar world, he was always certain of what he was supposed to be doing from moment to moment.

Between tutoring sessions, Michael shared a mid-day meal with Simbel, which consisted of bread, melons, leeks, beans, and a ration of wine. They would sit at a long table in a room that had a large window cut out along the length of the outside wall. It was a nice building, one of the few built out of a light colored stone, lit by the sun so they ate and studied by natural light. A young monk around Michael's age would come in around the tail end of their meals to prepare for the afternoon tutoring. Simbel would often motion to the food with her hand, to which the young monk would politely motion refusal and gratitude.

The monks never spoke, but after a couple of days, Michael decided he would find a way to make one of them talk, or at least laugh. One morning, an elderly monk strode into his room with a fresh robe and set his sandals in place. He turned to the small table to set out the facial paints and powders Michael was required to wear (Simbel had explained that he must make himself beautiful in the eyes of the gods, as they found ugliness distasteful). While the monk's back was turned, Michael slid the sandals aside. The monk glanced at Michael after arranging the makeup, then looked down and noticed the sandals were missing. Looking left and right, he found the sandals behind him and bent over to move them back where he thought he had put them. While the monk's eyes were away, Michael reached over and rearranged a few of the bottles on the table. The monk stood back up and stared at the table in frustration. Michael had now managed to put his robe on backwards like a hospital gown, and turned around and bent over to pick up his sandals, exposing his rear to the silent monk.

"Oh thank you! I was looking for those," he said, still bent over, and looked behind him at the monk.

The monk's eyes narrowed, his nostrils flared, and he gave Michael a swift kick to the rear. Michael tumbled forward and hit his head against the wall. Despite the pain, he fell over laughing. The monk flung his hands into the air and stormed out of the room. A few moments later, a much younger and much larger monk stepped into Michael's chamber. His smile was wide as he stared at Michael, cracking his knuckles and beating his fist against his palm. He looked like he could juggle cattle.

Michael was dressed and ready in less than a minute, making it to breakfast early that day. Clearly, he would have to try a different tactic.

A week later, a monk who was maybe a year younger than Michael came to mend a tear in his robe. Michael had seen her before, as she was the other pupil studying under Simbel. But, because she had taken a vow of silence, the two had never been introduced. She sat on a low stool, concentrating very intently on each and every stitch. Michael decided to put some of his new religious education to good use.

"You know," he said, "Rey, the sun god, came to me in a dream

JOURNEY OF THE SPIRIT MAN

last night."

The monk set her work down on her lap and looked blankly at Michael.

"He told me he was going to rise a little late tomorrow."

The young monk returned a skeptical look.

"Yeah, it's true. See, the people below the horizon worship a different god: Luna, the moon god. Anyway, the moon won't be on our side of the globe for a couple of nights, so Rey is going to stay over on that side for a few hours later so he and Luna can...well, of course you know what those gods do."

"You sound like an idiot," the young monk said. "Is this always how you speak?"

Michael started laughing. "I thought you weren't allowed to talk!"

"Whatever gave you that idea?"

"Don't you have a vow of silence or something?"

"Yes, a *self-prescribed* period of silence. I can talk whenever I want to."

"Oh." Michael thought a minute. He couldn't imagine keeping silent if he felt like talking. He was, after all, American. "Then why do you do it?"

"Do what?"

"Stay silent in the first place, if you don't have to."

The young woman smirked. "Job security. As long as I pull my weight, know my place, and choose my words carefully, I know where my next meal is coming from." With that, she returned to her work.

Was Michael the kind of person, like this young woman, who preferred to be secure and safe—even if it meant keeping silent or doing other things he didn't want to do? Or was he the sort of person who would risk his livelihood, or perhaps even his life, to be himself—to demand what he considered his rights? He wasn't sure. He suspected he was the latter but if he was in Aegypt long enough, he might become the former. Perhaps his character was less a product of his own wonderful self—as he'd always wanted to believe—and more a product of the environment around him.

It wasn't exactly a comforting thought, but there was some satisfaction in having entertained the idea. It didn't feel like something he would have contemplated before his strange journey began.

"So what's your name?" Michael said.

"You don't need to know my name."

"Why? It's not like—"

"If anyone heard you call me by name, they would suspect I have not been taking my vows seriously. So you just don't need to know it."

"Okay," Michael said.

Despite not knowing her name, he was glad to have at least some connection with someone around his age in this unfamiliar land—even if they never spoke to each other again.

A few days after his encounter with the young monk, Michael came across some small polished bronze mirrors among the priests' supplies. Later that day, he and the monk were sitting on the same side but at each end of a long table, listening to Simbel ramble on about the constellations or some particular cartographic error—Michael really didn't know what the woman was talking about. He slid one of the mirrors along the table to his friend, then used his own to reflect sunlight onto the table and motioned with his head toward Simbel, who had her back turned to them as she pointed to various markings on the map, or chart, or whatever. The young monk raised an eyebrow.

Michael found a nice target to the left of Simbel's head and directed a ray of sunlight there. As soon as it had caught Simbel's attention, however, the mirror was already under a stack of papyrus Michael was supposed to be using as reference material. When Simbel returned to the task at hand, the younger monk found a target to Simbel's right. They took turns distracting Simbel, until—

"Where are those lights coming from?" Simbel demanded, spinning around.

Michael looked around the room, trying to muster genuine, innocent confusion. "I don't know. I saw them too."

The young monk just nodded solemnly.

Michael looked out the window and found a possible source. "Ah, maybe it's reflecting off the Ciceron, the gift of our Most Radiant Cheron-Rey-Neteru."

Simbel looked out the window. The waters were unusually stirred up; an occasional glimmer of light reflected off their waves.

"Perhaps," she said, unconvinced. She pulled down a blind made of reeds, eliminating the source of her students' enjoyment.

A few days later, Michael stepped out of his room to find a bent and beaten bronze mirror at his door. He didn't know who left it there—he didn't think it could be the young monk—but he wasn't going to find out, and he wasn't going to give anyone a reason to do the same thing to him as had been done to the mirror. He started taking his lessons a little more seriously after that. The young monk also stopped talking to him. Perhaps she'd received a similar warning. Had Simbel sent that message? Did she know what he'd been up to?

Michael was learning something important about himself. He was growing more and more used to his new routine, his new life. If he stayed here long enough, he might not only adapt, but actually become Aegyptian. It wouldn't be a bad thing, necessarily, but, given that he did still intend to make it home eventually, the thought unsettled him a little.

In the evenings, priests escorted Michael to various temples to continue his education and participate in the worship. He had an evening meal in the banquet hall associated with the temple he happened to be serving at each night. He relished the nights that a little sliver of meat lay beside his plate as he ate with the priests. Despite the rather basic meals he had with them, he much preferred their company to that of the monks. The priests were a loud and boisterous folk, and as a part of their priestly responsibilities to enjoy their work, they were required to drink beer with their meals. After sampling what the priests themselves brewed, Michael wasn't sure he could go back to drinking filtered beer when he returned home.

He also enjoyed his time dining with the priests because it

afforded him glimpses of this vast empire's realm. It was the only time he could hear people speaking candidly about the state of the empire, and he felt he learned more from overhearing these conversations than he did during Simbel's lessons. Judging by the priests' discussions, he gathered that the empire of Aegypt was larger and mightier than he could have ever imagined. It stretched across half the continent and, on the back of slave labor, had become the wealthiest empire in the world. Enslaved laborers toiled night and day across the realm, planting, harvesting, and building cities which were unrivaled anywhere on earth. Michael wondered why he had been spared from similar toil, but dared not ask for fear he might be put to work in the fields merely for speaking out of turn. Punishments in this kingdom, he had learned, were swift and fierce.

"What do you get when an Ethiopian slave starts talking to a Hebrew slave?" a priest said at dinner one evening.

"What?" another said.

"Not enough work done!" They both laughed and spilled their beers. He shuddered as he thought of his conversation with Mark only a few...he wasn't sure how long ago. Was it weeks? Months? In any case, he remembered how he had told Mark that everybody wanted to be his friend, but he didn't have the time to put up with them.

"They're not your friends," Mark had said. "When your glory is gone, they'll be gone..."

Could the same be true of an entire empire?

During these meals, Michael asked questions about the kingdom and its religion and the priests didn't mind answering. He was surprised to find out that many of the priests were actually deists. They didn't believe in the specific gods of Aegypt. They didn't believe that Pharaoh Cheron-Rey-Neteru was a god either.

"Michael, Michael." An older, very jovial priest threw his arm around Michael's shoulder. "The Pharaoh is not a god; he is a *representation* of the great god Rey. So we respect him as a god, being the representation of a god, even if he is, of course, a poor representation. But we do not see him as the god."

The priest must have read the confusion on Michael's face, because he went on.

"It's like us, the priests. We represent the spirit of the Pharaoh. Our liturgy actually says we are the Spirit of the Pharaoh, but trust me, if you cut me with that knife you are using on your meat, I will bleed, not the Pharaoh. It's just a representation."

"So...you don't believe in any of this?"

"Not in the same way as the common people do."

"Then why do you teach it?"

"People need a religion. It's something they depend upon. You may say that people could better use their time and resources on other things, but trust me, if they don't occasionally give an hour of prayer here or a sacrifice there—uh, better yet, think about it this way: you cannot always count on the harvest, but you can always count on the celebration of the harvest. People need an outside perspective on their own lives. It helps them realize areas where they may need to improve themselves to improve their life altogether. This is why we discuss how lifestyles negatively affect the crops during the celebration of the harvest. When you say that, someone who had some poor yields on their crop is going to start thinking about all the times he went to the apothecary without a real need, or all the women he was chasing, and then, trust me, he's going to have a better harvest the following year. Because he'll change his behavior!"

Though Michael considered himself non-religious, he found himself surprisingly bothered by this admission of social engineering by someone who was supposed to believe it the most.

"But if you don't actually believe in any of this ritual or religion," he said, "then doesn't that mean it's all fake?"

"Absolutely not! Michael, it could all be real and legitimate and all well and good, but it's not about what the priest believe—remember, we are just a representation—it's what's going on right in here." He poked Michael in the chest. "When that man I spoke of comes to the celebration of the harvest, resolves to change his life for the better, and then brings in the first fruits the following year of his large and now plentiful harvest, this," he lifted his arms and turned this way and that as if to encapsulate the whole temple, "is more real than anything you and I can ever know."

It was different with Simbel. Simbel was a true believer. Michael struggled with that initially. Could he respect somebody who believed in something that he knew, with every bone in his body, was false?

Once, during a lesson, he asked her about it indirectly. "Have you always followed the Pharoah?"

"All my life, I have known that he is our leader," she said. "I have always respected and honored the Pharoah."

"What if you're wrong?"

She considered his question carefully before she responded. "If it turns out I am wrong, if it turns out we are all wrong, then I will accept it. But I know it is never wrong to honor and respect those who make decisions on our behalf. If they make wise decisions, we celebrate them. If they make poor decisions, we hope and pray that they learn from their mistakes. If they do not..." She paused. "No matter what your role in life," she said at last, "whether you are a leader or a slave or a priest or just an ordinary citizen, there are always ways you can resist unjust rule."

She left Michael to his thoughts. It was then that he realized there was more to her than met the eye. She might seem as though she only followed tradition, did as she was told, did not think for herself. But instead, she thought about who she was and who others were and considered the most orderly way to bring change, while keeping harmony in the kingdom.

She had some wisdom, Michael realized. Wisdom he could learn from.

Chapter 13

On the banks of the Ciceron, Simbel taught Michael that Cheron, the great Pharaoh, had a lifelong obsession. As his father Ankh-Marcus lay dying, Cheron had had a vision. The best way to ensure the survival of all would be to conquer Death. Therefore, he would devote his life and use all of his power to become the Destroyer of Death.

He called upon all the oracles and all the seers in the temples, and set them searching for his answer. Submitting himself completely to the fanatical belief that his cause was just and achievable, he set out to create a nation that would uncover the secrets of immortality. A man of great intellect and passion, he inspired his people to believe in his cause, and his obsession had directed the nation's course. It was a war machine, conquering other nations and enslaving their peoples to provide the manpower necessary to pursue the increasingly complex designs called for by the oracles and the engineers and the alchemists. The more ambitious the Pharaoh's attempts became, the more fervently he believed he was nearing the end of his quest. He would find Death and destroy it, then rule an undying utopia for eternity.

The Pharaoh's greatest project was a quarry being constantly deepened by tens of thousands of slaves. Already it took an hour to cross on foot, and grew larger by the day. A steep road spiraled to the bottom along its sides, always filled with workers ferrying loads of dirt and stone up from the quarry floor far below. Even with the ant-like hordes of dust-caked slaves working day and night, the work had already taken decades. To feed them, the Ciceron itself had been re-routed by dams and canals and made to serve the Pharaoh by watering crops tended by thousands more slaves. The purpose of the project was to uncover the Abode of Death, which the oracles had told him was to be found in the bowels of the earth beneath a certain spot.

The Great Pharaoh Cheron had proclaimed his cause most vital to the empire's existence, and thereby justified any expense whatsoever. His use of power was without limit or mercy, driven by one simple ethic: anyone who refused to be a part of his plan was a defender of Death, and therefore an enemy of all humanity. All those enemies were graciously granted an opportunity to embrace Death.

In the years since Cheron came to power, the people were on the whole much happier than they had been before, Simbel assured Michael. The empire had endured great hardships before Cheron, because everyone was pursing their own interests for their own gain. But Cheron had brought a common dream to all the people, to conquer and destroy Death.

"By giving His people hope that we might all enjoy immortality," Simbel said, "our great Pharaoh Cheron-Rey has given meaning to our lives."

On a particularly hot afternoon, Michael was taken by two of the silent monks through a long underground corridor to the main building of the Great Temple. He was escorted through halls of increasing splendor, and then made to wait just outside the Central Chamber of the Pharaoh. Though he could not see into the room, Michael could clearly hear what was being said. One voice stood out. It was a deep, resonant voice which he had not heard before.

"My dreams tell me I am close to finding Death. What my dreams do not tell me is how I am to kill it."

Another voice spoke, which Michael recognized as Simbel's. "It is in the Scriptures, Radiant Eminence. The Sacred Scrolls tell us:

> Out of the Ciceron will come
> A man to go before the Sun.
> From Death's Abode he shall return
> The answer to the seeking one."

"I know that scripture as well as you," the first voice said. Michael heard something metal clattering to the floor. "Riddles! Do the Scriptures tell you when this man will be here?"

"I believe I do, Pharaoh," Simbel said. So this other voice belonged to none other than the Great Pharaoh Cheron-Rey! Michael tried to picture the man behind such a powerful voice—tall, imposing, dour—but he dared not peek into the room.

Simbel went on. "The scriptures also say:

> When the moon closes its eye
> The journey will be finished.
> The end a new beginning,
> The beginning a new end.

The astronomers tell us there will be an eclipse of the moon tonight. I feel that you will have your answer then."

"Tonight," the Pharaoh said, his voice hushed with awe. His powerful steps echoed across the chamber and Michael heard the rasp of the shutters being flung aside to reveal the city beyond. "Can you hear it?" Cheron said. "The screams of Death dying, crying in anguish... It will be the ultimate victory for our empire. Can you hear it?"

Simbel spoke with great reverence and sincerity. "Mighty Pharaoh, only you are great enough to hear it. We humble servants must rely on the words you give us."

"But what of this man you mentioned? The one who comes this very night? Do the scriptures say anything more of him?"

"Attend this, Radiance," Simbel said. "This is why I have come before you today:

> Out of the Ciceron shall come
> A man whose god is not anyone.
> Traveled through the healing earth,
> He goes before the mirrored truth
> To share Death's secret with the Sun."

There was a moment's pause, and then Cheron spoke in a hushed voice. "Have you found him, Simbel?"

"I have found a man," Simbel said. "He was discovered lying in the mud of the Ciceron, and he told me he had been washed from the high mountains by the rains which heal our valley each year. He said he worshipped no god, and are you not the Sun? If he precedes you where you must seek, will he not bring back your prize?"

"Bring him to me!" Pharaoh ordered, and in seconds, the door burst open and Michael was brought before the mighty Cheron-Rey-Neteru, Pharaoh of Aegypt, god of the Temple, and ultimately the Destroyer of Death. Two guards pushed him to his knees.

"What is your name?" The Pharaoh looked him over as if examining a sacrificial lamb.

"Michael Seymour," Michael said, suddenly very afraid of what this towering figure might be capable of. The Pharaoh was every bit the larger-than-life man he had pictured. He seemed to take up the entire room with his sheer presence. He possessed a gravity entirely his own, and everyone nearby seemed pulled in by it, unable to look away. Cheron communicated with a barely-perceptible nod of his head what would have taken a lesser man many words to express: he found the specimen before him acceptable.

Cheron placed his hand on Simbel's shoulder. "Simbel, I am close to fulfilling my dreams, thanks to you. My gratitude will be eternal. When life ceases to submit to its once-ultimate end, you will sit at my right hand for ages upon ages."

Before she could respond, one of the overseers Michael had seen at the quarry burst into the room.

"Your Radiance!" he said. "Your Radiance!"

With a lazy gesture, Cheron indicated he may speak.

The man threw himself on his face before the Pharaoh. "It is there, Radiant One, just as you said it would be. We have found the Abode of Death!" Tears of joy coursed down his face. "It is a great stone dome, and when it was struck, it rang like a bell. The slaves are clearing a passage for Your Radiance as we speak."

"Then the world is mine," Cheron laughed. "And eternity will be mine. Bring the horses and light the way with torches. Make the night shine like day so I may see that which I have sought for so long. Go!"

The news of the discovery spread quickly throughout the city.

People rushed from their homes to fill the streets that led to the pit. The courtyard of the Great Temple was a chaos of people yelling orders, horses screaming as they were pulled and whipped into their places, and people running in all directions. Women carrying jars of oil ran forward to permit the torch slaves to dip their torches in preparation for the descent into the pit.

As the sun set, Cheron and his advisors mounted their golden chariots and began the parade through the city. Michael was placed in an ornate cart and driven alongside Cheron and Simbel. The people screamed out their praises and their prayers to their leader as he passed among them, and they threw thousands of little funnels made of woven papyrus reeds before him as he proceeded. A brilliant full moon appeared in the sky, and seemed twice as large as ever before. Then the screams of the people increased to a mad howl, and their hopes and fears drove them to groveling tears as the sky began to darken.

As thrilled as any of his people, Cheron thrust his arm up to point at the moon. One side had begun to darken, as though the orb was evaporating.

"Just as the Scriptures read," he pronounced. "When the moon closes its eye, the journey will be finished."

"It is written!" shouted Simbel above the roar of the crowd.

Torches blazed in the pit, illuminating the long winding road to the bottom with a ghastly flickering light. As they hurried round and round, the sky above grew ever darker. By the time they reached the bottom, the moon was almost fully eclipsed. Only a sliver remained, and it was vanishing quickly.

The torchlight revealed a half-excavated, perfectly smooth dome of polished rock. A short distance away, a phalanx of armed men kept the excavators on their knees and held swords at the ready. Judging by the trembling among the kneeling men, all of them would have run away in fear if not for the guards.

One of them leapt up and ran toward Cheron.

"Pharaoh, Pharaoh! Spare us! Let us flee!" he screamed. "I heard voices screaming in pain. We have discovered the gates of Hades."

Cheron glared at the man. "We shall harbor no fear. Kill him."

A soldier stepped forward immediately and cut the man's throat.

Cheron stepped down from his golden chariot. He walked over the body of the slain slave and approached the dome. The structure stood the height of three men and was about forty paces in circumference, a sealed dome of polished granite. Cheron ran his hand along its perimeter, searching for seams, but apparently found none. He placed his ear to the dome and listened, but again seemed to gain nothing from this. The air was still and silent as people waited for their Pharaoh's command. Overhead, the final sliver of the moon disappeared and the darkness beyond the reach of the torches became entire. Cheron motioned to one of the guards to bring him a heavy worker's pick. He took the handle in his hands and swung the head against the dome. Beneath their feet, the ground shook as the dome rang like a bell tuned to the lowest possible note a human could hear.

"Make a hole big enough for a man to walk through, here," Cheron said, pointing to a small spot in the dome where his pick had chipped off a single flake of granite.

In seconds, the slaves were driven forward and their tools began to ring against the stone again and again. The noise of metal against rock echoed around and around the bottom of the quarry until it became a single, constant tone, sounding endlessly through the night. As soon as one slave grew too tired to perform his task, another took his place. Though they kept at this for a long while, the moon did not reappear and the darkness did not abate.

Inch by inch, the rock surrendered to their relentless assault, until a chisel finally penetrated to the other side. With a sound like a dying scream, the dome seemed to exhale a burst of compressed gas. The slaves closest to the puncture howled in terror, dropped their tools and backed away. They were whipped, clubbed, slashed with swords, and replaced with fresh labor.

"Keep working!" shouted the guards, their own fear kept in control only by whipping the slaves.

A few minutes later, the doorway was complete. Cheron peered inside, but no matter how many torches were brought, the darkness inside swallowed up all the light and nothing could be seen.

"It is time to fulfill my destiny," he said. He drew his sword and stepped toward the gaping darkness.

"Wait, Great Pharaoh," said Simbel, grasping the ruler's forearm. "Send another man in first. Let him tell you what he finds." When Cheron looked at her sharply, she added, "It is for us that I ask this, not for you, Great Pharaoh. We, your people, cannot live without you."

Cheron sheathed his sword and pointed to a slave. "Send him in."

The man shook, and though he knew there was no appeal, he fell to his knees. "Please have mercy!" he wept.

Cheron kicked dirt at the whimpering man. "Here is your mercy. Kill him." A soldier swiftly did as he was asked. Cheron pointed to another slave. "You, then. Send him in."

The man closed his eyes, whispered a prayer, and walked courageously into the entrance, where he was instantly swallowed by the blackness. They waited. No one moved, until suddenly a tortured voice cried out from the dome.

"No! No!" The slave stumbled out, his hands covering his eyes, and collapsed at Cheron's feet.

Cheron snatched the slave's head up by his hair. "What did you see?"

Unable to answer, the slave simply looked into the Pharaoh's eyes. The fear Michael saw in the slave's face was unlike anything he had ever witnessed before. Not even the poor souls in Gehenna had displayed such raw, existential terror. Cheron drew his sword to kill the man when Simbel interrupted him.

"Great Pharaoh, why use a cowardly slave to do the job of a brave volunteer?"

"You are right, Simbel," Cheron said. He released the slave, who collapsed to the ground and continued staring into space, mouthing words he was unable to speak.

"Which of my faithful will not fail me?" Cheron called out. "Who will enter Death's Abode in my name?"

After a moment's pause, one of the soldiers stepped forward.

"I will serve, my Life-Giver," he said.

A few minutes later, however, he too staggered from the dome, babbling incoherently and shuddering with unthinkable dread.

Cheron shook his head, then turned to Simbel. "Well, High Priest?"

Simbel pointed to Michael. "Bring forward the one who has been taken from the Ciceron, the one who has no god, and let him go before Cheron-Rey into the Abode of Death."

In seconds, Michael was brought before the blackness.

"You have come from the Ciceron," the Pharaoh said. "You claim the name of no god, and you have come through the mountains whose rains heal our land. Are you the man who has come to bring me the secret I seek?"

"I'm just looking for a way home," Michael said. "I miss my family, my home, and the woman I love. I have traveled through Gehenna, the Holy Mountain, and Paradisa. I don't know if I'm the one you need, but, well...here I am."

"Enter," Cheron said.

"What if the answer I find is not the one the Pharaoh seeks?"

The guards and slaves were shocked to hear someone question the Great Pharaoh. Cheron was silent. He looked at the dome, then looked back at Michael, pondering. At last, he simply pointed toward the entrance.

"Go!"

Michael did as he was told.

As soon as he entered the darkness, a white light blinded him. When his eyes finally adjusted, he saw he was surrounded by mirrors. From every angle his reflection looked back at him in this strange, half-real space. Then the images began to move, to change, to become something other than a direct reflection. In the eyes and expressions and flesh he saw himself—who he really was, not what he wanted to project to the world—come to life. Scenes from his life flashed so rapidly in the myriad mirrors, and were so unflattering, that he had to close his eyes. But even with his eyes closed, he could see as clearly as if they were open and the truth was too much to bear. Every wrong he had ever committed. Every prideful, boastful moment. Every bit of flagrant selfishness. Every ounce of harm he had caused those around him. All of this danced in his mind not as an image, but as if he were actively reliving each and every one of these events.

He wept.

To his left, Mark's killer appeared in one of the mirrors, taunting him.

"Come on, rich boy! What are you afraid of?"

As Michael stared at him, his visit to Gehenna ran through his head. The cross, the sword, the rage that had almost driven him to do something unthinkable. But that was so long ago now—it felt like it had happened to a different person.

"You're trying to bait me," Michael said. "But it won't work. I don't hate you. I feel sorry for you. Go in peace. I hope you find what you're looking for."

The mirror shattered and fractured into the silicone grit from which it had been made.

In another mirror, Michael saw himself pushing past his parents and fleeing the house. His mother sat on the bed weeping and his father sat to comfort her.

"Mom! Dad! I'm so sorry," Michael cried out. "I know I've been a selfish child, but I'm going to try to become a man you'll be proud to know."

The mirror shattered and turned to dust.

The next mirror showed only Wendy. She stood, arms at her sides, watching him warily. She did not speak, and the longer she went without speaking, the more her silence pierced him.

"Wendy," Michael croaked. "I don't deserve your forgiveness. You're special, more special than I'll ever be. And someday you'll meet somebody who will treat you the way you deserve. I am so sorry."

The mirror fell and shattered into a million pieces.

Michael turned and saw himself in another mirror, back at Fat

Manny's.

"Seriously, have another beer, man," mirror-Michael said. "This isn't going to take long." He heard himself say the words as though he were speaking them today, this very instant, and the words cut straight to his heart.

"Mark!" he nearly screamed, his voice cracking. "I'm so sorry. You were right...so many times. You've always been a better man than me, and I only hope I can someday live up to all that you knew I could be."

The mirror exploded.

A more horrifying image appeared behind it. Not one from his past, but one from what might be his future. He was sitting in a wheelchair, his body and his mind destroyed by the ravages of disease. The figure sat motionless, uncaring, unfeeling, dead even though he was still alive. No one came to visit him. No one called or sent him letters. He was entirely and eternally alone.

Michael turned away as if he could will the picture to be false. That couldn't be his future, could it? He could still escape it if he just... if he just....He took a deep breath, turned back, and faced the grim specter head on.

"Live, dammit," he said. "Smile, or cry, or yell, or whatever you have to do. This is the only life you get, so just live while you're able!"

The image twisted in on itself and the reflection shattered.

A thousand more faults came to life in the mirrors, and as he faced each one and conquered it, he knew he could deal with the next, and the next.

"I can change," he told the last of the mirrors. "I can forgive. I can be forgiven."

At last, after this final pane burst into nothing, no more mirrors appeared. Michael was left in silence, amid a field of broken glass. Despite the sound of blood pounding in his ears, he felt at peace—something he realized only then that had never felt before in his entire life.

He walked out of the dome, ready to face Cheron. He knew that Pharaoh would be astonished to see him, calm and collected, unlike the other men who had gone before him. When he emerged into the night, no one spoke. A thousand torchlit faces watched him as if he were a wild animal, waiting to see what he might do next. Michael turned to the Pharaoh and nodded.

"Well? What did you see?" Cheron said.

"We must speak alone," Michael said.

Cheron looked at the moon. The eclipse had begun to pass. The moon was becoming brighter and brighter by the second. Would the passageway close once the eclipse ended? Judging by his worried expression, Cheron seemed to be thinking the same thing.

"Everybody leave," Cheron commanded.

"I cannot leave you, my Pharaoh," Simbel said.

"There is nothing you can do," Michael said.

Cheron nodded, and the quarry erupted with activity as the swarm of people hastened to obey their Pharaoh and depart. In moments, Michael found himself alone with Cheron. The Pharaoh looked at him impatiently.

"Speak," Cheron said.

Michael considered his words carefully. He sensed—no, he knew—that a single wrong move here would cost him his life. How was he supposed to convince this man that his entire life's purpose was impossible?

"What you will find in the Abode of Death," Michael said, "is a mirror. A mirror which tells only the truth. In that mirror, you will not see Death, nor a way to destroy Death. Instead, you will be taught, in a very painful way, that you should not fear Death, but rather fear not having lived. To live, we must not flee from the world, but face it, and to do that, we must be able to forgive. To forgive each other and ourselves. I cannot tell you what you will meet in the dome, oh Great and Mighty Pharaoh, but if you seek to know the truth, you will have your chance tonight."

"You dare tell me Death cannot be defeated?" The Pharaoh pulled out his sword.

Michael did not flinch. "You asked only for the truth, Cheron. I have given you what you asked." He waited. Would Cheron kill him then and there or would he keep him alive another day? After everything he had seen inside the dome, all the lessons he had finally understood in that unreal place, he desperately did not want to die.

Cheron's voice trembled as he said, "I have created the greatest army that has ever walked the earth. I have conquered countless nations and I am sworn to destroy Death. If this dome holds the truth, as you say, I will face it. If this truth breaks me, as it did those men who went before you...then I am not worthy of leading this empire. If I come out screaming, I am less than a slave and I ask only that you kill me." He removed his armor and threw his sword upon the ground, then entered the dome without a step of hesitation.

Michael sat on the fresh-turned earth to wait, and on the tiers of the spiral road above him, the thousands of slaves and soldiers sat also. Silently, the long hours passed. People began to murmur. Had the Great and Mighty, Most Radiant and Glorious Pharaoh Cheron-Rey-Neteru fallen to the powers of Death, Lord of the Underworld? Some people silently wept, restraining their cries of misery with only a tremendous effort. Predawn grey bloomed across the sky. Then, just as the Great Radiant Rey broke over the eastern horizon, Cheron stepped out of the dome into the clear golden light of dawn. The people watching from above cheered ecstatically. The Pharaoh seemed even taller and more regal than he ever had, and he looked at Michael with both suffering and compassion in his eyes.

Cheron approached Michael, to be heard over the deafening roar of what seemed like the entire empire screaming for their leader.

"I have been a fool," he said. "I have followed a nightmare instead of a dream. Michael Seymour, whoever you are, I promise you—and myself—that these blood-stained hands will never take another life."

Michael bowed before the Pharaoh. "A most honorable resolution, Your Radiance."

Cheron shook his head. "No. No more 'Radiance,' no more 'Mighty Pharaoh.' From now on, call me simply...Cheron the Good."

For a moment, Michael wondered if it was really that simple:

declaring oneself good and thereby becoming good. The only way to know for sure would be to measure the change in Cheron's actions, but perhaps the name would encourage him. Perhaps it would serve as a permanent reminder of what he was meant to be.

"Well, Cheron the Good," Michael said with a smile. He looked to the throngs of people watching from above. "What are you going to tell them?"

"I will tell them..." He paused for a moment. "I will tell them I died. During my time in death, I had a long quarrel with Death that lasted eternal ages. By my own wisdom, I was able to not only persuade Death to return me to the Land of those who Live, but to also be gracious and merciful to those in the Land of those who Live. No longer will Death lurk around every corner and behind every rock, but Death will claim only those who have lost a great amount of blood, those who have a damaged or aged vital organ, those who have been afflicted by a disease or poison, those who have been greatly burned or have fallen from great heights, those who have succumbed to infection or starvation or dehydration, or such things. No longer will people die from looking at a sundial for too long, or from stepping upon the Pharaoh's shadow. Death is what makes us human, and we are not to defeat it, but to accept it so we may fulfill our lives. Today the Conqueror of Death has died within the dome. I will begin my new life by spending my vast wealth to pay these people to fill this pit, and to construct over it a great pyramid to remind us of Death's finality."

"Did people really ever die from staring too long at a sundial?" Michael said.

"They did before today." The Pharaoh smiled.

Michael nodded. The Pharaoh still wasn't being truthful about what he'd seen, or acknowledging his own role in the violent and sudden nature of death in his empire, but perhaps this was still a step in the right direction. Michael could only hope. Pharaoh Cheron raised both his arms as though in triumph to his people, and another mighty cheer made the deep pit shake.

"Come with me, Michael Seymour, and we shall get to work,"

the Pharaoh shouted over the roar. "I shall begin by freeing all the slaves, and offering them all good wages to stay here and work."

"Oh Great Radiance!" Simbel came running, falling prostrate before the Pharaoh. She groveled and crawled backwards to stay in front of Pharaoh. "What have you to proclaim to us? We wait upon your words with all our lives! Speak to us, Mighty—"

"Enough, Simbel," Cheron the Good said. "I have seen the truth about myself, and I admit it has not been an easy one. Stand. Do not grovel before me any longer. I am no master of yours."

"But Pharaoh—"

Cheron stopped her with a wave of his hand. "You are a good person, Simbel. And loyal. But you must not throw yourself at anyone's feet, now or ever again. Get up, I say. We have a future to build."

Simbel staggered to her feet, her eyes wide and round. She scurried along ahead of Cheron and Michael as they made their way to the chariots. She would serve Cheron well, Michael knew. If anyone could hold him to his new title, it was Simbel.

"Now what of you, Michael Seymour?" Cheron said. "Anything you want here in my kingdom, you may have. Simply say the word and it is yours."

"Thank you, Cheron, but what I really want is to find a way home."

As Cheron the Good stepped into his chariot, he called Simbel to his side. "When we reach the top of this ridiculous hole, see to it that Michael Seymour is given a suit of our best light armor, a fresh horse, as much food and water as it will carry, and two soldiers to accompany him wherever he wishes to go. He is free."

Simbel bowed before Pharaoh and mounted her horse. She rode up the path ahead of them, clearing the way for their chariot. As Michael and Cheron passed the people, they fell in line behind them, forming a long procession marching out of the spiral of death. When Michael and Cheron finally reached the top, the new day was radiant. The sky was blue and the smell of honeysuckle filled the air, welcoming the parade back to the world.

Michael remained one more day and night to join the celebration hosted by Cheron the Good following his announcement that every man and woman in his kingdom then and thereafter was a free citizen of Aegypt. The following morning, Michael dressed himself in the simple and comfortable attire of an Aegyptian light cavalry-man, mounted the horse Cheron had given him, bade a sincere fare-well to Pharaoh and Simbel, and departed the Pharaoh's complex. He permitted his soldier escorts to accompany him for a few miles thanked them for their help, and told them to return to their homes.

In the emptiness of the desert, Michael found a road. Not well traveled, winding into the most desolate region of the desert. Michael took a deep breath, summoned his resolve, and struck out along the path.

Chapter 14

The land seemed more familiar the farther Michael traveled. Red dunes like a sea frozen in high swells stretched in all directions beneath a cloudless indigo sky. He heard no sound at all except the wind and the *shiff* of his horse's hooves in the sand. He rode on.

For a time, he wondered if he had made the right decision in leaving Aegypt. He had a place there, he had the admiration of the people, and besides a part of him wanted to see Cheron make good on his promises. While it wasn't the world he'd grown up in, maybe it was a world he could grow used to, accept, and even love. He still had half his food and water rations. It was not too late to turn around, rather than continuing on, a nobody, a wandering soul trekking through the desert, part of some demented artist's world as she sketched an endless sea of air and space.

But no.

The old Michael Seymour would have stayed, would have reveled in the glory heaped on him by his proximity to the Pharaoh, friends and family back home be damned—but he wasn't that person anymore. He wasn't sure, exactly, who he was, but he finally understood who he wasn't.

Still, plodding through that vast nothingness dominated by sand and sky, he felt empty, hollow, and lonely. Rainless clouds the color of dust piled up above him. It was like being buried alive beneath an ocean that had not seen water in millions of years. If he were to die here, he would dry out and wither away in only a few years, and even his DNA would become denatured and unidentifiable; there would be nothing left to testify to the existence of Michael Seymour.

He shook the thoughts from his head and pressed on. No matter what, he had to get home. He had come too far to end his journey in this desolation. And when he got home, he had to do all he could to prove he had changed. He had to make his actions match the new person he believed himself to be. He may have lost Wendy forever, and Mark was gone—but he could still be a better person for them. He could be a better son. He could let Mark's parents know he would be there for them, no matter what. He could be a good man.

Michael traveled for days without rest. His horse persevered night and day, night and day, through valleys, between canyons, along the ridges of mountains. Michael vowed that he would not stop until he reached his destination, though he did not know how far it might be, nor if he could reach it at all. He rode through the sun's searing heat as it swerved drunkenly across the sky, setting and rising at seemingly random places along the horizon.

Michael's mind wandered over all the strange places he had been. The lost souls in Gehenna serving out eternal punishments resembling the very lives they lived. Yamani leading her people into a new age of peace and prosperity. Paradisa, now abandoned, left to dissolve into the forest. And Aegypt, an entire empire forced to accept the inevitability of death and flourish from that acceptance.

The sky rippled slowly and gently with color, in a much less chaotic fashion than it had when he first entered this fantastic reality. The world seemed to have arrived at something close to an equilibrium.

Mirages played in his mind, visions of fertile valleys, flowing streams and serene rivers with green slopes and lush pastures. It was springtime and the fields were full of tall blue grass. Then, in the waves of grass, he saw a single black blossom. When the vision faded, something remained in its place: Mark. He stood atop a dune, holding something black.

Michael drove his horse to a gallop. He came to a skidding stop with a grin on his face as he saw the tie in his best friend's hand— the same tie he had buried so long ago. He dismounted and his smile widened. There, beyond Mark, stood the adobe gate. The way home.

Mark returned a polite smile, but said nothing.

Michael tapped his horse's rump to send it homeward, and turned to face his own portal home. He put his hands against the door and found it was vibrating softly, like the purring of a sleeping cat. He found himself trembling in tune with it. He could finally go home.

But Mark still hadn't said a word.

"Mark?" Michael said.

Mark's smile faltered but he said nothing. He just looked at Michael as if from very, very far away.

"Mark, we can go home," Michael said.

Mark closed his eyes for a moment. "Michael."

"What?"

"I can't go back. I died. But you're still alive. You can go home." His voice cracked as he stared at the adobe gateway.

"No, no we can fix that," Michael said. "Come with me." Somehow, after all the fantastical events of his journey, the idea that Mark could cross back into their world with him had stopped being an idea and become something more like a fact, a certainty. Even if he was still a temperamental ghost appearing just to chastise him, Michael wanted Mark in his life so badly. He felt his breaths turning shallow as that possibility slipped away from him.

"I can't," Mark said. He took a deep breath and handed the tie over to Michael. "I know you want me to, but that's not possible. I died. I can't be in that world anymore."

"But the gate is right here, Mark. It's right here!"

Mark only shook his head. As much as he wanted to fight it, Michael knew Mark was right. There was no way back for him.

"I don't want you to be gone," Michael said. "I don't think there will ever be a time I don't miss you. But I hope you find happiness here. I really do."

Mark's smile returned. A small, sad smile. "I'm really proud of you," he said. "You've grown so much, and I get the feeling this is only the beginning for you. You have so much life ahead of you, and so many great things. For me, though, this is it." He seemed oddly at peace when he raised a hand and said simply, "Goodbye Michael."

A soft breeze stirred across the desert and when it caught Mark he dissolved into a million grains of sand swirling away and away across the dunes. Disappearing into the vastness.

Michael couldn't breathe. After all this, after everything he went through, this hurt the most. But he had to keep going, for Mark. He wrapped the tie around his arm, approached the gate, and felt the slight vibrations of the door against his fingertips. The lightest push swung the gate wide open and in a blink Michael was sucked inside. He went tumbling through an incomprehensible void. Static electricity enveloped his body and his hair stood out in all directions. A swirl of wind stripped his tunic and cuirass from his body, leaving him naked except for the tie, and spinning to the edge of consciousness.

The door slammed behind him with a mighty boom and an all-encompassing darkness surrounded him.

Then a beam of light cut through the blackness, a fissure through which Michael could see. Through that small crack in the shadows, he saw a broken man curled in the fetal position on the ground, his skin ashen, his body scratched and bruised, his hair dark with blood. At first, Michael thought the man was dead. Then the pitiful figure turned his head and Michael realized he was staring at himself.

Michael reached out a hand and helped his battered self to his feet. An instant later, a surge of energy ran through their bodies, reuniting the fragments of their soul. The world burst into a shower of light. Michael fell through space, through constellations, stars, planets, clouds of nebulae and galaxies. The kaleidoscope of colors exploded, blinding him, and he spun dizzily.

When the spinning stopped and the dizziness cleared, he realized he was back on the mountain path overlooking the fertile valley of the Rio Grande. The Organ Mountains towered above him, and the voices of friends and family seemed to echo from the rocks.

He was home.

Soon he'd see his parents. He could apologize. He could make good on the promises he had made to himself, to be a better son. He could be a better man for Wendy, even if she decided not to give him another chance.

He touched his head and found it gashed and painful to touch. His face was covered in dried blood. His white shirt was stained and torn. Finding no other serious injuries, he stood, took a deep breath, and started towards home.

ABOUT THE AUTHOR
George Mendoza

George Mendoza was born in New York City in 1955. At the age of 15, he was diagnosed with a rare, incurable, degenerative eye disease, fundus flavimaculatus. Effects of the disease caused him to lose his central vision, keeping only a gray foggy fringe on the periphery. In the center of his view, he sees what he calls "kaleidoscope eyes"—intense and changing visual images of fiery suns, brightly burning eyes; and colorful pinwheels. These spectacles almost never leave him, not even when he lays down in darkness to go to sleep.

A man of vision and courage, George went on to become a world-class runner and Paralympic contender. In 1980, he broke the world record for blind athletes, running the mile in 4 minutes and 28 seconds. In the early 1990's, he began to paint full-time. Ironically, Mendoza's paintings spring from the loss of his eyesight and a very special vision that took its place. He had grown increasingly frustrated by his dancing colors, which would not leave him alone. He spoke to a priest at the Holy Cross Retreat House in New Mexico. "Paint them," the priest said. "Make designs, pictures from them."

George Mendoza remembers physical sight, and so his works derive from visual memories intertwined with dreams, visions, and emotional experiences, meaning Mendoza paints both figuratively and abstractly. His work then transcends the physical world, exploring the spiritual, the mystical, the playful, and sometimes the darker nuances of the human spirit.

Mendoza works full time as a writer and an artist. Currently, his exhibition "Colors of the Wind" is a national Smithsonian affiliates traveling art exhibit. He lives in Las Cruces, New Mexico, and is founder and president of the Wise Tree Foundation, Inc., a nonprofit corporation for the promotion for the arts. He is a motivational speaker and is currently developing a play based on his children's book *Colors of the Wind*, a biography of his life written by J.L. Powers and illustrated using Mendoza's artwork.

Learn more at www.georgemendoza.com.

CPSIA information can be obtained
at www.ICGtesting.com
Printed in the USA
LVHW040520050522
717887LV00001B/39